T0023041

BUDDHA
WAS A
COWBOY

ALSO BY JUNIOR BURKE

The Cold Last Swim

BUDDHA WAS A COWBOY

A NOVEL

JUNIOR BURKE

GIBSON HOUSE PRESS

CHICAGO · FORT COLLINS

This is a work of fiction. While certain public figures and established cultural elements are mentioned, names, characters, story, setting, institutions, and incidents are wholly imaginary.

GIBSON HOUSE PRESS
Flossmoor, Illinois; Fort Collins, Colorado
GibsonHousePress.com

© 2022 Thomas Bishop

All rights reserved. Published 2022.

ISBNs: 978-1-948721-18-9 (paperback); 978-1-948721-19-6 (ebook)

Library of Congress Control Number: 2022934040

Cover and text design by Karen Sheets de Gracia.
Text is set in the Alternate Gothic and Adobe Caslon typefaces.

Printed in the United States of America
22 23 24 25 26   5 4 3 2 1

For Fred Koller,
songwriter and bookseller

A monk asked Hsiang Lin,
"What is the meaning of Bodhidharma
coming from the West?"

Hsiang Lin replied,
"Sitting for a long time becomes tiresome."

ZEN KOAN, CIRCA 1125

PART ONE
LIFTING

CHAPTER 1

Before

Like most institutions of higher learning, Parami University was a world unto itself. The word "universe" is contained in university, although Parami, at six hundred students, was more the size of what is commonly referred to as a college. Perhaps it was because Parami began modestly, holding classes over a health food co-op in Pearl Handle, Wyoming, that when it was granted accreditation, it announced itself more grandly than it was.

A sizable institution sprawled nearby, Southern Wyoming University. Many students who attended SWU were unaware that Parami existed, being more concerned with football, Greek parties, and suds-guzzling in the area of Pearl Handle known as the Peak. Parami's reputation was more national and even international, widely regarded as a leader in what is termed Mindful Instruction.

Its origins were indeed mindful, founded by Lawrence Timmons, an Australian-born Columbia professor of comparative religions who left the U.S. in the late nineteen-sixties and journeyed to Tibet, where he stayed until the early seventies. Upon his return to America, he published *This Is Now Here*—part memoir, part self-help—gaining him a following that many termed a cult. Timmons moved to Pearl Handle, then a back-to-the-land enclave, and began lecturing above the co-op, and that is when his followers—most of whom had been ignited by the sixties and were, in the aftermath, tasting its ashes—fastened upon the notion of a proper school.

The late, controversial filmmaker Willard Pettibone was a Timmons enthusiast and, at Timmons's invitation, would come from New York to Pearl Handle to conduct workshops, eventually founding Parami's Arts Program. Many noted writers, musicians, dancers, painters, and performance artists were enlisted to participate because Pettibone's fame shone brightly and, as Pettibone would say upon proffering invitations to prospective guest instructors: "You can sleep with the students."

ON A JULY afternoon in 2007, as the Keyholders of SWU were inducting young men into their membership, Parami students were engaged in an unrelated protest. No one in either of these disparate assemblies knew of any event that day beyond the one they were attending. Yet each took place, commencing at the same hour, Sunday at 2:00 p.m., both out in the open, separated only by a waist-high cyclone fence.

The Keyholders were a creation of head coach Burt McCandless, who'd been an all-American cornerback at the Air Force Academy and, in his third year of coaching SWU, was still looking for a winning season. That was why, the previous fall, he introduced the practice of praying in the locker room before the game, praying in the huddle when it was third and long, then ultimately praying at the beginning of each set of downs.

The prayers at first were general, asking for universal help and guidance, eventually making the leap that Jesus of Nazareth was invested in the fortunes of the SWU Coyotes. In postgame interviews, whenever a win was registered, a player might proclaim that: "My personal Lord and Savior Jesus Christ was listening to our prayers today, especially during that pass to the flats that Conrad grabbed for sixty-seven yards."

An SWU associate professor of political science pointed out in the

Pearl Handle Recorder that Southern Wyoming, being a state-funded institution, might look into whether on-field Christian prayers transgressed the separation of church and state. A controversy erupted, resulting in Coach McCandless promising that prayers, when offered, would be less specifically dispatched. He was, however, inspired to form the Keyholders, a Christian-based, male-only organization whose mission statement included "doing battle against the secular humanism and encroaching feminism that infests our society and threatens the future of America and its children."

At first, the Keyholders thought the cameras were for their initiation ceremony. When they determined that the media were instead documenting the activity across the way, they began to simmer. Reverend Thaddeus Fogarty of the Pure Life Church, their guest speaker, spotted Harvey Gluck, a feature writer from the *Recorder*, and summoned him to the fence.

"What on God's earth is going on over there?"

"A protest against last fall's election, the ban against same-sex marriage."

"What's newsworthy about that? You're just promoting a bunch of freaks and their deviant lifestyle."

"All due respect, reverend, but we've already covered the Keyholders. No new angle there."

Fogarty fumed away.

Gluck was about to rejoin the protest when Mitchell Amritt, a thirtyish, part-time Parami groundskeeper, copiously pierced and tattooed, in sleeveless T-shirt, tight jeans, and calf-high motorcycle boots, appeared beside him.

"Is that really Thaddeus Fogarty?"

"Yep, that's him."

"The dude Bush gets on the Oval Office phone so he can pray with him?"

"The very one."

"Funny," said Mitchell with a smile. "I know him as Nick. I see him every other week or so."

"Where do you see him?" asked Gluck.

"Motel rooms, mostly. He's one of my regular tricks."

When the story broke in the *Recorder*, Reverend Thaddeus denied having ever met Mitchell Amritt. But the *Denver Post* picked up on it, then the wire services, and it went global with CNN and the twenty-four-hour news shows, beaming murky yet undeniable images of the reverend, captured on Mitchell's cell phone, in leather pants and spiked dog collar, devouring a Burger King Whopper out of a plastic dish.

Within seventy-two hours, Fogarty's Pure Life Church accepted his resignation. The scandal prompted a statement from the Bush White House: "Contrary to what has been reported, at no time during his administration did the president rely on the counsel of Reverend Thaddeus Fogarty. In fact, the president participated in one conference call when he was amassing anecdotal information from a wide range of spiritual leaders regarding the state of faith within the United States."

In the "faith-based community," meaning the evangelical Christian Right, Fogarty's fall was seismic. Mitchell Amritt's account, meticulously recounted on all the major news and talk shows, included not only bondage and domination, but crystal meth and crack cocaine. Fogarty's colleagues, charged with investigating his conduct, scarcely had a precedent. Three weeks after the avalanche of revelations, Fogarty was declared by them to be "one hundred percent heterosexual," a pronouncement met with such derision that it had to be amended to: "Reverend Fogarty is now ready to denounce homosexuality in himself and others and is eager to assume an exclusively traditional and sanctified relationship with Lindy, his wife of fourteen years."

Pure Life Church, on the plains near Valmont, Colorado, boasted an active membership of twelve thousand. Plans were underway to break ground on an undergraduate college that would produce Christian leaders who would meet the challenges of the new century. In the six months following the scandal, attendance at Pure Life had fallen thirty-six percent.

All discussion regarding the proposed college were removed from the agenda of the Strategies for Evangelical Fellowship, an annual national Christian leadership conference held in Dayton, Tennessee.

CHAPTER 2

Aaron

Aaron Motherway, for fifteen years, since receiving his MA in American Lit from UCLA, had been a scriptwright. That was a distinction he'd arrived at, different from being a screenwriter. Screenwriters wrote for the screen, seeing their work funded and developed and produced. Scriptwrights wrote for the page.

That is not to say one couldn't make a living at it. Hollywood was lousy with those who had written a feature-length script that had seized the fancy of an agent or producer, and lived well above the mean national income, rewriting or polishing existing scripts by other writers, a tiny percentage of which made it to the Cineplex or to one of the boutique television entities.

And this was the minority. Far more common were those who toiled as waiters, drivers, clerks, you name it, who perpetually had a script going that wouldn't make it past an agent or producer or development head but would languish on hard drives and in drawers and dusty boxes, never to be read by more than the select friends and contacts of that writer's circle. Aaron Motherway lived between those two equations; never having a film produced yet landing the rewrites and polishes that would see him through the fiscal year.

He'd started out with one of the tri-lettered conglomerates but then pitched in with Valerie Easterbrook and Associates, who had ferreted those assignments for him for the last decade, although, with the proliferation of streaming, the work was getting increasingly less lucrative. The associates alluded to in the company name were an ever-revolving stream of young men and women who would serve as Val's assistant for six or nine months before moving on to other employment.

Aaron's friend Freddy Smoltz had been a scriptwright for a mere ten years, and he and Aaron shared Val as an agent. Despite all evidence to the contrary, Freddy remained undaunted, never having anything sold or even optioned, generating two feature-length scripts a year, supporting himself as a telephone solicitor of varying content.

Like Aaron, Freddy had no wife or partner, no child to support. He lived alone and appeared to have no intimate relationships. There was a suggestion that he frequented low-end Hollywood strip clubs, but that was as much as Aaron knew, or wanted to know, about that aspect of his fellow key-pounder.

Val Easterbrook believed in Freddy, as she did all her clients, but was growing weary. Val mentioned more than once to Aaron that she longed to return to her beloved New Hampshire and invest in a small business, something solid and predictable, a hardware store perhaps. Aaron never commented on these reveries, but they were not unfamiliar to him. In his years in Hollywood, he'd heard at least three other such scenarios from agents or producers, always involving some bucolic embrace of the past, and always including a hardware store. Embedded in the unconscious of those whose survival depended upon dreams on paper seemed to be a longing for something steadfast and essential; drill bits that fit, fixtures that would fasten without resistance, pristine nails to be pounded into accommodating slats of wood.

But somehow, Freddy Smoltz beat the odds. He wrote his first romantic comedy, about Stefan, a fellow much like himself, who becomes engaged to the heiress to a petroleum fortune. A grand wedding is planned in Houston. An elaborate, yearlong, round-the-world honeymoon is charted out. Then, while sorting through the RSVPs, the bride-to-be gets cold feet. The wedding's off. The groom is devastated. Out of guilt, the heiress concedes to Stefan's solitary request: let him go on the honeymoon, all expenses be damned, by himself.

That was the first ten pages.

The script unfolded in a series of desirable locations: Sydney, Singapore, Tangiers, Paris.

In each locale, Stefan encounters a different beautiful woman who is captivated by his tale of loss and abandonment and becomes quite eager to give herself over to him for a brief fling so that he can mend his shredded heart.

For the third act, it's back to LA for a chance meeting with Laurie (the heiress's name). But now Stefan is worldly and confident, and Laurie falls for him in a way she would never allow herself before. The story ends with them running in the rain to Beverly Hills City Hall to state their vows before the justice of the peace.

The script was called *Leap of Fate*. Val sold it to Paramount for one hundred fifty thousand dollars, a modest sum by industry standards, but one the execs deemed fitting for Freddy Smoltz who, in their parlance, was a "first-time writer."

Aaron—anyone—might have thought that Freddy would be overjoyed at this turn of events. But like a child who covets a toy only to abandon it after a session or two, Freddy was strangely agitated. "Why this one?" he whined to Val and Aaron during their celebration at the woefully lit Mexican restaurant that Freddy had, for years, frequented. "Why not *Hollow Point* or *Queen's Ransom* or *Serial Saint*?"

Val sipped her third Margarita. "Timing, my dear. You finally had what they were looking for, at the moment they were looking for it. These execs see each other all the time, in—and mostly out of—the office. They wanted a romantic comedy, and that's what you came up with."

"I've run the numbers," said Freddy, with more than his usual degree of misery. "With this sale, I've made less than 15K a year for ten years of writing. That's not accounting for a decade of inflation. At twenty scripts, that's less than seventy-five hundred a shot."

Aaron couldn't recall whose idea it was, Freddy's or Val's. But the seed was planted that night, in that undistinguished restaurant, at that very table.

The next day, Freddy changed the title of *Leap of Fate* to *Change of Heart*, *Solitary Honeymoon*, *Frequent Flier*, and seven others. Stefan and Laurie became Lyle and Samantha, Sam and Lucy, Stuart and Lorraine. Val sold the script to three major studios as well as seven independent production companies, each for the ballpark one-fifty.

Shortly after, she and Freddy split a seven-figure pot and said farewell to Hollywood. Val headed for hometown Portsmouth where she bought a fourplex; Freddy to Scottsdale, Arizona, a town that seemed attractive. He purchased a sprawling ranch home, as well as an outskirts establishment that he refurbished to accommodate exotic dancing.

This was all done with Val's repeated assurance that none of those scripts would ever get shot. Each executive who championed their purchase would be out on their ass inside of two years. Other writers would be brought in to rewrite what was deemed good enough to purchase, cloaking the content even deeper. Options would be agreed upon only to lapse at term. Nothing would ever come to fruition because so rarely anything did. They were safe; they'd hopped into the getaway car and sped away.

Aaron Motherway had been gleefully apprised by each of the perpetrators of the fraud they'd committed. Freddy and Val were certain that Aaron wasn't going to utter a word, given that all three shared a similar loathing of the Business. Trouble is, a writer knows a good story when they hear it. So, while not a word passed his lips, Aaron decided to write about it. When he sat down to do so, the customary *FADE IN* was replaced by this sentence: *In the past ten years, Sean Patterson had written twenty screenplays.*

Aaron went on writing, populating his hard drive in the manner that Kerouac attacked his scroll, days and nights of caffeine and scarce sleep and refused invitations and avoidance of TV and phone.

Three weeks later, he had eighty thousand words he called *The Sell Out*. He no longer had an agent, so he cold-queried ten in New York and two of them emailed back and one of those returned his call and that was who placed the manuscript.

The novel didn't make the best-seller list but was well-reviewed, most significantly in the *London Observer:* "It is not misplaced to regard Mr. Motherway in the tradition of Nathanael West and Budd Schulberg and other authentic voices who have possessed the courage and artistic wherewithal to put the garish absurdity of Hollywood under a microscope."

Aaron was overjoyed with the reception but worried that ultimately his efforts would cause Freddy and Val to be found out.

He needn't have troubled himself. After the initial flash of publication, Aaron surmised that no one at the aforementioned studios or production companies had read his book.

CHAPTER 3

Journal as Verb

Daniel Coyne sat in his Lexus SUV on a tree-lined street in Pearl Handle, Wyoming, outside the massive house he'd shared with Regina, and gazed at the dim light from the second-story bedroom. They were up there, Regina, his wife, and Philip Pristley, the worm who had corrupted her being. Every night, Daniel would drive over from the hotel and sit here, knowing too well what was taking place upstairs. Tonight was different, however. Tonight was Daniel's birthday. Regina had sent a card, a soupy, watercolor image whose printed message said: *Whatever your path in life, know I will be there to support you and cheer you on.*

Daniel wanted to vomit all over it and send it back.

He'd scarcely been able to work these past, what had it been, five weeks. His company, the one he'd founded sixteen years before with Regina's money, was in good enough shape that it could run without him. Agra-gen was its name and it had been a pioneer in genetically engineered agriculture, Frankenfood, as it was disparaged. The environmentally astute in Pearl Handle would view this as a controversial enterprise, so he kept his business low-profile, the colorless offices out on the plains, betraying no indication as to what might be going on inside.

What he and Regina were much more public about was their

philanthropy, conspicuous sponsors of the Pearl Handle 10K Run plus the local film festival, and both served as Timmons Trustees at Parami University.

That proved to be the undoing of their otherwise perfect union. Regina became intrigued with Parami's Arts Program, taking a personal enrichment class with Pristley, Journal as Verb, which led in some unfathomable way to Daniel sitting outside his own house, gazing up at the amber-lit room—bedroom, his and Regina's—in which his beloved wife, partner, confidante, and most enduring friend was swapping DNA with some lowlife bohemian.

The betrayal started, it seemed, innocently enough. Regina hadn't voiced an enthusiasm for quite some time and, a few weeks into Pristley's workshop, the tap was turned on. Pristley assigned each of his students to keep a notebook at hand should inspiration visit them when they were not in proximity to a computer. Regina was dutiful, purchasing several, each a different color, all of the Moleskine variety. Soon, Daniel never saw her without one.

After several weeks, Daniel found himself growing curious. This was accentuated by an unsettling remoteness Regina was exhibiting. "You seem a bit preoccupied," Daniel said one evening, during an especially quiet dinner.

"I'm not," said Regina, almost with a start. "What would make you say that?"

"Just . . . you seem a little distant."

Regina moved some food listlessly on her plate. "It's probably just . . . the journaling. It causes you to create a world within yourself." She looked up at Daniel in advance of raising a bit of kale to her lips. "It makes you live two lives at once."

The following evening, while Regina was taking an uncharacteristic nocturnal shower, Daniel noticed she'd left her current orange notebook on the bedroom dresser.

He couldn't.

That was hers and hers alone. She'd been so protective, often walking around with it, the way one might clutch a canteen during a hike through dry terrain.

He couldn't.

Except he'd left the bed and was standing at the dresser, an ear tuned to the water pounding in the adjacent room. Now, his hands on the notebook, Daniel turned back pages, a burglar deftly configuring the digits of a safe.

Midbook, at the final written page—the back of a page—he was looking down at the blue ink written in Regina's distinctive hand, the sheet to the right of it unblemished. His eyes closed in on the looping scrawl. Four brief lines at the bottom, off by themselves.

High Coo, it said, clearly a title. Then a trio of lines:

> *I'm speechless, Philip*
> *But I don't mind*
> *As I keep you sweet in my mouth.*

In his Lexus, Daniel felt a wave of panic spreading through him, over him. He'd never struggled with anything like this, always had a grasp on his emotions. Since Regina's betrayal, his body, slim to begin with, was getting slimmer all the time, devoid of appetite, invaded by sensations he didn't recognize, over which he had no control. At first it was episodic terror, but now a low, insistent alarm had taken up residence and had the power at any moment, in any circumstance, to spill over and consume him.

Lately, he'd been often overcome by things he'd heard about, read about, seen reported on television—seemingly ordinary persons shooting or stabbing or bludgeoning a spouse, a sibling, a coworker—events previously remote and implausible.

Driving in Laramie one afternoon, he'd impulsively pulled off the road and into the parking lot of a pawn shop whose banner out front announced Gun Sale! He went in and, in a disembodied state, bought a Charter Arms .38. Now in the glove box, nestled atop the thick Lexus manual, Daniel eased out the gun and felt its weight fill his hand.

Once he shot Philip Pristley—and he could, he knew it, right in the forehead—he'd need to kill Regina and then himself. A waste, as his life up to this point had been perfect. Parents, loving and supportive, education unfolding with well-deserved prizes and scholarships. From their first meeting in college, he and Regina were a team, her trust fund launching Agra-gen, right product at the right time, multiplying and spreading like a swarming hive. But now everything was ruined.

Daniel turned on the satellite radio, hoping it would distract him. Scanning, he came across a sonorous voice. Plaintive and powerful all at once, its tone seized Daniel as he took in what was being said.

"Nobody knows more about making a new start than yours truly. I had everything, and then had everything taken away. Oh, some of it was my fault, not paying attention to the things I needed to pay attention to. My wife, Lindy, Lord knows I neglected her. Now I need to ask myself, was I truly doing the Lord and Savior's bidding, or was I just doing things for my own ego and vanity, saying, 'Look at me, look how power-ful I am, how wise.'"

To Daniel, the voice was like a song he'd needed to hear, at last playing for him.

"Well, I was brought down all right, but now I'm back, and this time, I can say I'm truly committed to the Lord's divine mission. I've got no secrets. No shadows. What you see is what you get. And that's why I'm telling you tonight that no matter where you are, if you really want to make a new start, now is the time."

Daniel's response had begun in his ears and his brain but now it consumed his body, that message, that voice, a glimmer on the horizon.

"They say there's no time like the present. I say, there's no time *but* the present. Bow your head, fold your hands and say, 'Reverend Thaddeus, carry me to the Lord.'"

Daniel heard himself say: "Carry me, please carry me."

"For I'm ready to come through Reverend Thaddeus and give myself over."

"I'm giving myself over."

"This is not a passive prayer. This is a statement that from this moment onward, you are recruited by Reverend Thaddeus. The forces of darkness are fierce. The power of darkness is enormous. *Regina's up there* . . . That's why you need to become a vessel of holiness, of integrity, who will not be swayed by the legions of Satan, which can be sweet but will ultimately send you down in flames . . . *debasing herself* . . .

"So, if you're with me—if you're truly with me, then strap on your provisions and prepare for the journey . . . *consorting with pure evil* . . . Are you ready to join the Lord's legion?"

"I'm ready."

"Are you ready to sign on with Reverend Thaddeus?"

"Ready to sign with Reverend Thaddeus."

"I no longer have a church, no longer have a place to hang my hat except on these airwaves and at ReverendThaddeus.com . . . *No longer afraid, nothing to be afraid of* . . . But still I'm ready for the liftoff, are you coming with me?"

Daniel wiped away tears, then, hands still gripping the pistol, body contorted, he knelt on the plush leather seat.

"I'm coming with you."

He felt a power swirling in him, some heavenly vacuum cleansing him, instilling strength and renewal. Like some movie sped up, he was behind the wheel, tearing away from what could have been his rival's murder, Regina's murder, his own suicide.

Reaching Basin Boulevard, along the south side of the Pearl Handle River, Daniel came upon a tiny bridge. He activated the button and his window descended. Switching the weapon to his left and dominant hand, Daniel was rolling over the bridge when, with all the force swirling in him, he flung the pistol at the river.

CHAPTER 4

The Chat Room

Aaron knew he didn't have another book in him. Writing *The Sell Out*, the sheer athletic accomplishment, the pure act of blind will, was not to be franchised. It was like an ordinary individual who, walking on the street, comes upon a fellow human writhing beneath an automobile and—fueled by adrenalin—hoists up the chassis. Where that power came from—how it had been marshaled—could not be repeated. That person was not going to give their life over to snatching drowning souls from eddying waters or hauling petrified children from blazing houses. No, Aaron wasn't a novelist; he had written a novel, and those designations were in entirely different columns.

The questions "what are you writing now?" and "what are you doing next?" were flung at him in all kinds of circumstances. The answer, although he never uttered it, was some version of "nothing." Having channeled a considerable work that carried more substance than any script he'd written or rewritten or put a shine on, he couldn't stomach another screenplay. He'd built a house; he saw no point in following up with a blueprint and leaving it at that. Yet he had no premise for a book, no notion of how to even approach one; a state of artistic amnesia. But the questions kept coming, as did the invitations.

As a fledgling scriptwright, Aaron scarcely was invited anywhere outside his limited circle. As a recognized novelist, he was now on some kind of list, invited to openings and cultural events that were prestigious but invariably loud and crowded and flashy. Such was the opening of the Los Angeles River Photographic Exhibition at the downtown Museum of Modern Art.

That LA even had a river was not generally known. But an up-and-coming photographer named Molly Li had documented it each day of the previous year and Aaron felt it sounded like an interesting project.

At such a gathering, the crowd takes precedence over the work itself, and this was no exception. A number of famous faces were in attendance. Aaron, there by himself, was accustomed to being solo. He did see a couple across the way whom he'd known before *The Sell Out* was published, Geoff and Ellie Waterman. Aaron went over and they shared a warm but meaningless exchange, before introducing him to Dodie Vincent.

Aaron didn't watch much television but had seen her local interview show, *The Chat Room*. Being in Los Angeles, her subjects were primarily from film and television, often actors, but just as often producers and directors, as well as California political figures.

"Good to meet you," Aaron said, shaking her hand.

Had Aaron ever considered it, Ms. Vincent was shorter than he would have presumed, as onscreen figures often are. She had styled white-blonde hair and a slim figure wrapped in an elegant, silver-shaded dress.

"Is it?" said Dodie Vincent with an unreadable smile.

"Beg your pardon?" replied Aaron, over the din of the crowd.

"*Is it* good to meet me? We tried to get you to sit down with us while your book was hot, and you never returned our calls."

Aaron had no direct knowledge of what she was talking about. "That must have come from the publicist. I wasn't too eager to be interviewed."

"You weren't too shy to go on KABC and KUSC."

Aaron glanced at the Watermans, both of whom were smiling. "Those were radio. Not everyone looks good on television."

Dodie Vincent offered a smile that appeared genuine. "Explanation accepted."

Aaron lingered with the three of them for a time until they separated.

He was surprised the next afternoon when Geoff called and said, "Look, Dodie just got divorced and isn't seeing anyone. She'd really like you to give her a call."

DODIE VINCENT WAS from Norman, Oklahoma, and started out writing for *Variety* before transitioning to TV. Her five-year marriage had not included children, and she was four years older than she claimed to be.

Aaron determined the age discrepancy during one of their conversations and she reluctantly copped to it, saying, "Look, Motherway, you can't tell anybody. A girl needs every year she can get in this town. I'm not kidding. If word gets out, I'm holding you responsible."

To Aaron, their relationship was intriguing, if frustrating. They would reach a level of intimacy, even tenderness, and the next day they'd be at back at square one, with Aaron forced to negotiate when they might see each other again. A light, easy evening and a close, intense night might be followed by a distant phone call, only to be followed by a perfume-scented letter from Dodie with statements such as: *My life was so empty before you arrived. Come in, my lover. Take me and let me take you to the depths and to the heavens.*

Aaron would never reference these missives, which seemed to come from some hidden place Dodie only accessed on occasion. Whenever Aaron wondered why he was hanging in, given such uncertainty, a letter would arrive as though it were the 1800s. *My life had no music until you placed your fingers on the keys. Be steadfast, my dearest. When we reach our mutual destination, you will not be disappointed.*

Dodie rarely asked what Aaron was up to. He was somewhat relieved, keenly aware that life after *The Sell Out* was still a big question.

Dodie lived in a cabin-like structure in West LA. She didn't seem to spend much time there, at least not with Aaron. When he'd come by to pick her up, she was usually set to bustle out the door. Overnights together were at his place in Los Feliz. That's why Aaron was surprised when she invited him to come to dinner the following Sunday.

"I'm not much of a cook, Motherway, but I've got a lasagna recipe I'd like to take a shot at."

Aaron arrived at the appointed hour, 7:00 p.m., cradling a forty-dollar bottle of Chianti. He pressed the bell and, when it failed to induce any buzzing or chiming, rapped on the door. When this didn't generate any movement inside, he knocked again and as he was doing so, the door swung open. Dodie stood in what looked like a kimono, dim light and shadows behind her.

"Didn't we agree you'd always call first?" was how she greeted him.

"I thought we were having dinner."

A look crossed Dodie's face. "You got it wrong, Motherway. I wrote it on my calendar for *next* Sunday."

They stood there a moment. Then Dodie said: "I'd invite you in, but I went whale watching all day and I'm feeling a little woozy. You know, from the sea and all."

Aaron muttered an irritated response because he knew he hadn't gotten it wrong. He strode back to his car, the lights of Los Angeles glowing beyond, feeling done with Dodie Vincent.

In LA, an environment that placed paramount importance on what one could or chose to drive, Aaron owned a two-decades-old Jaguar XJ6 whose forest green original paint was waning. Still, Aaron loved it when it wasn't in need of some repair or adjustment which, increasingly so, was the case.

Clearly in no hurry, his drive back to Los Feliz did not require the hectic navigation of the LA freeway system. Aaron drove so frequently in Los Angeles that the familiar streets and intersections had lulled him into complacency. As he glided along a dark stretch of Melrose, one of those phantom blocks between Western and Vermont, he paused for the stop sign, then eased into the intersection. The crash came from the left, and Aaron was jolted right and onto the floor on the passenger side.

There was little sound in the aftermath, just a settling to a new and damaged state, glass tinkling, steel reconfiguring into contorted, chaotic shapes.

Aaron lay stunned and crumpled, knowing he was hurt, trying to determine how hurt he was. The front of his shirt seemed damp, but he wasn't hurting there. His collarbone and left shoulder felt dislocated, the pain spreading like an oil spill. He wanted to stand, needed to get out of the car. With his right hand he groped for the door handle and, when he found it, pushed down. Moving through the pain, he shoved against it with his right shoulder and tumbled out onto the pavement.

He lay there a moment. Tried to rise but couldn't, collapsing miserably. There seemed to be no one around, no one who'd stopped on the street, no one who'd emerged from their residence to see what caused such a commotion.

Above and beyond him, Aaron did hear something. Footsteps. They kept getting louder and closer until, in the dim light of the intersection, he was eye level with a pair of gleaming leather shoes. That they had been crafted in Italy absurdly entered his mind.

"How bad it is?" came a baritone infused with some indeterminate accent.

Aaron took a moment. "Can't move my arm. Shoulder's all twisted."

"I will give you money," the voice declared. "Cash money, if you agree not to call LAPD."

What? Aaron's mind tried to right itself. "We have to call," he managed.

"Three hundred dollars."

Some bills were pressed against Aaron's right hand.

"No," Aaron uttered.

"Five hundred."

"No, goddammit, help me up."

The bills were pulled away, and Aaron heard himself cry out as the full weight of the man forced the left side of Aaron's neck and shoulder into the pavement. The pain in his left arm and shoulder intensified as though a blazing torch had been put to them. When the grinding pressure finally lifted, Aaron again heard footsteps, this time moving away. A massive engine fired up and a set of tires squealed before spinning from the scene.

Aaron lay there, no longer wanting to get up. Soon there were fresh sounds and voices.

A pair of white running shoes appeared beside him, their owner addressing someone in Spanish. Aaron could translate only the last word.

Ambulancia.

AARON LAY IN back, on a stretcher. A siren screamed above him, and he glimpsed blue and red lights, flashing and twirling. How many times had he been in traffic and eased over to make way for an ambulance speeding from behind? He'd rarely, if ever, considered that someone lay inside, having just had an accident or suffered a seizure or succumbed to some severe illness. But on this night, at this moment, he was the one taking his turn in the barrel.

The female attendant, looking down on him from above, appeared impassive. They were slowing now, taking a turn, coming to a halt, as Aaron experienced a new sensation. His left shoulder felt as though it were dissolving. He tried to move his left arm but felt like that limb was being erased. Now it crept over his left side, descending to his waist and steadily down his left leg. Someone, he assumed it was the driver, flung open the door. This unseen person and the other attendant pulled Aaron out the back, where he was not so gently thrust onto a gurney.

Out in the air, Aaron felt a wave of panic that the feeling of his left side disappearing was going to spread. He was still on his back, staring straight up. It appeared that the sky was being opened like some momentous book.

In Los Angeles, the sky was something he rarely considered, since you couldn't clearly see the stars at night, just a reflected glow from the unnaturally illuminated city. But no, there were stars on this night— thousands, countless numbers of them—yet each appeared individual and distinct. Then, with the suddenness that it appeared, the magnificent cosmos was blacking out, star by star, atom by atom. Aaron felt the darkness sweep over him. *Don't go away,* his mind cried out. *If you go away, then I'll go away and I'm not ready.* The stars that remained, half of what had appeared, remained glowing and sparkling in brilliant contrast to the blackness that held them.

With the parts of him that could still experience sensation, Aaron became aware of rolling forward. Emergency Entrance glowed the red light above the glass doors. "I look really frightened," Aaron said to himself. "I wonder what they're going to do to try and save me."

Aaron could see what he was seeing and say what he was saying, because now, floating above, he watched with detachment as the attendants pushed his prone body across the glare of the lobby toward a set of elevators.

CHAPTER 5

Moses

The Reverend Doctor Stamford Moses, all six foot four of him, stood beneath the shower in the Holiday Inn, Colorado Springs, water flooding his bearded face, shoulders, chest, forearms; his entire mahogany-shaded frame. He imagined that the water was baptizing him, cleansing him to meet the challenges of the new day, which hinted to be challenging indeed.

He'd been summoned by Roger Bayne Whitney, founder and driving force behind several Christian and conservative groups and organizations, the most prominent being the Creationist Alliance, based here in the Springs, a region so populated with fundamentalist Christians, it had become known as the Evangelical Vatican. Why Roger Bayne Whitney who, it was said, always insisted on being referred to in triplet, wanted to talk was, in Stamford's mind, still in question.

Stamford reluctantly turned off the water, toweled, and swiped on deodorant. He slipped into the dress socks, highly starched shirt, suit, and tie he'd arranged carefully on the armchair. His shoes were polished to a high gloss. It was eight thirty, and his morning was already two-and-a-half-hours old. He'd worked out for an hour in the gym, glanced at Fox News in his room, ducked downstairs for the so-so complimentary breakfast during which he thumbed through *USA Today*.

Had he any inkling of what this meeting was about, he would have prepared for it, but Roger Bayne Whitney was considered to be furtive, even mysterious. Many more knew about him than had seen him in the flesh. Within the rarest evangelical circles, Roger Bayne Whitney was said to like that just fine, the world he was avoiding being treacherous and foul.

Downstairs once again, Stamford crossed the lobby and stepped out into the October air. *Bracing.* He'd heard that word before as it applied to atmosphere but had never really experienced it. But that's what the air was on that morning; thin and close, substantiating that on solid ground you were more than six thousand feet above sea level.

A car was waiting—a latte-shaded Chrysler 300—with a blonde young man in a navy blazer poised beside it. "Reverend Moses," he beamed.

Stamford nodded. The kid lunged for the rear passenger door and swung it open. Stamford climbed in. *Here we go.*

Stunning mountains loomed in the distance. This was another term Stamford, who'd never been in the West, had often heard but never experienced until now. The mountains sat like a low cloud formation. Nothing like this back in Iowa, where Stamford currently lived, or Florida, where his childhood was spent after his family left the Bahamas. No, these were major mountains, the genuine article, and they loomed.

The office building was tucked within a cluster of parkways at what appeared to be the edge of the city.

Upon entering, he found that the environment was muted, thin gray carpet and beige walls that seemed flimsy, almost temporary. An indistinct hum from nowhere in particular.

Stepping into Roger Bayne Whitney's unmarked office, Stamford was greeted by a silver-haired female receptionist-secretary around seventy, who wore a bright red pantsuit and ushered Stamford into a slightly larger and equally sterile space without the customary offer of coffee or tea or bottled water.

Roger Bayne Whitney received Stamford in a wrinkled blue and white pin-striped shirt, sleeves hiked to the elbows. His maroon tie was knitted cloth, not refined like Stamford's silk. In his sixties, he was broad, no, hefty, with a gut that could politely be referred to as ample. This was the man he'd heard so much about? His gray, off-the rack trousers were belt-less. Roger Bayne Whitney would not have seemed out of place on a used car lot singing the praises of a pre-owned vehicle.

Twenty minutes in, Stamford still had no notion as to why he was there. But when he felt unclear and uncertain, he did what he'd long ago learned to do when handling a confounding situation. He sat and listened.

"Being at a secular, liberal arts college and not a faith-based institution, you may think that no one in our movement has been following your career, Reverend Moses. But I assure you that's anything but the case."

Something about the way Roger Bayne Whitney said this unnerved Stamford, like a switch had been flipped and he was in the presence of a man he'd, until that point, underestimated. Roger Bayne Whitney leaned forward on his bare elbows and asked: "How frankly can I speak with you?"

Stamford knew he was about to learn the purpose of his visit. "As frankly as you wish, sir."

"That Thaddeus Fogarty scandal some years back . . . "

Stamford nodded.

"Threw a damn wrench into everything, excuse my language. We were set to break ground on a four-year college up in Valmont. Promised to be the crowning achievement of my career, turning out upstanding Christian Troops into the world for at least this next century. But with the beating we took in the liberal press, we've been off course ever since. We need to make up for lost time."

Again, Stamford nodded.

"I know you haven't yet been to the evangelical conference we hold every year down in Dayton, Tennessee."

"Right, I've never attended."

"Well, something very interesting took place at the last one." Roger Bayne Whitney smiled, clearly savoring the memory. "No, not interesting, *fascinating*. A recent convert from up in Wyoming, Daniel Coyne, was there to talk about genetic food engineering, with which he's been extremely successful. When it came up about the college we'd wanted to build in Valmont, this Coyne fellow asked an extremely compelling question."

Roger Bayne Whitney paused dramatically. Stamford had the thought that if the man had been holding a cigar, he'd have taken this moment to indulge in a dramatic puff. "This Coyne fellow said: 'Why start a school from scratch; why not just *take one over?*'"

Roger Bayne Whitney cackled in a way that startled Stamford. "After that, I had our Essence Center run a thorough workup, as I immediately pegged Coyne as an invaluable asset. First thing we did was snatch him away from Thaddeus Fogarty, damaged goods if there ever was such a thing." He let go a harsh laugh. "In fact, the Essence Center exists because, after the disaster with Fogarty, we need to know the true and exact nature of every last soldier in the movement." He trained his gaze on Stamford who, again, felt a wave of power and intrigue emanating from Roger Bayne Whitney. "Turns out, this Coyne's on the board of some hippie-dippie college up in Pearl Handle. How on earth it ever got accredited is beyond me. But it did, back in the nineties. Brilliant thing is, you seize control of a private institution, you don't need to go through the accreditation process, which can take years. Hell, you don't even need to buy it or build it, you just replace the curriculum."

Roger Bayne Whitney leaned back and smiled. He'd said his piece and now it was time for a response. But Stamford's thoughts felt tangled and all that formulated was: "Respectfully, sir, what does this have to do with me?"

BACK IN GREENSBORO, Iowa, Stamford told his wife, Delsey, what Roger Bayne Whitney had laid out. Delsey was enthusiastic, as Stamford assumed she would be. "I'll go," she declared. "There's never been enough color around here to suit me."

"From what I gather, there's not a lot of color in Pearl Handle, Wyoming."

"Well, it strikes me as an opportunity. You can get out of Development, which is looking more and more like a dead end. Unless I'm missing something, you've never been a college president."

"*Presider* is what they call it. Back when they started, they dreamed up different names for things. It doesn't bother you that Roger Bayne Whitney and company are just using me? They think these libs out there won't say no for fear they're not being inclusive and progressive."

"Everybody uses everybody, Stamford, you know that."

"The whole time sitting across from him, I kept thinking, how many people of color does this guy know? How many has he *ever* known? Has he ever had anybody who isn't white to his home?"

"We'll just put in a couple years, then you can apply for the presidency of a real university. Maybe even one that's historically Black."

Delsey was onboard. Now all Stamford needed to do was break it to Madlenka.

Like most serious transgressions, this one started under some veneer of decency. Madlenka worked in Benefits, and Stamford had gone to see her about including vision in the family health plan.

"Your eyes not working?" Madlenka asked, wrapping the question in her Hungarian accent. She boldly held his gaze. Scarlet hair and emerald eyes, Madlenka was certainly delightful to look at. On that particular day, she wore a turquoise dress that clung to her sculpted frame.

Stamford all but dashed out of her office.

They would see each other after that and there would always be some undercurrent accompanied by vague flirtation. At an alumni celebration, Stamford was on his own, as Delsey invariably shunned such occasions. Madlenka showed up in the company of the assistant rugby coach who, in his mid-twenties, was at least five years Madlenka's junior.

Stamford pouted, standing beside the punch bowl, feeling some unnamable emotion across his chest and in his gut. Seeming to sense his discomfort, Madlenka eased away from her date and came over, clutching a plastic cup of white wine, which Stamford had the impression was not her first of the evening. "Good to see you, Doctor Moses."

Stamford, not thinking, said, "What are you doing here with that dummy?"

"He asks me," she chirped, the tense decidedly Eastern European. "And how right would it look if I show up here with the man I much prefer?"

The affair, Stamford's first, had been surprisingly easy to manage. When a clerical position opened up in his department, he urged Madlenka to apply and saw to it she was selected.

They kept their assignations limited to lunchtime, always at Madlenka's condo. While intimacy had been a sure and steady feature of his marriage, what he and Madlenka shared was nothing but hot, crazy lust. From the instant the front door shut behind them, they'd fling off their clothing and wrap themselves in each other. In bed, of course, but also on the sofa and the floor and the occasional countertop.

Stamford felt guilty—because he *was* guilty. He wrote a sermon, The Totality of Conduct, which he delivered at a Student Worship Service, declaring that the Lord measured all deeds, be they good or glaringly wrong. If the scales leaned in the favor of wholesomeness and virtue, you'd still be admitted to heaven. At least, Stamford hoped, salvation worked something like that.

To break the news of his departure, Stamford invited Madlenka to lunch at Applebee's, on the pretense of going over some business. Far from certain how she would react, he was relieved to be moving. The kind of heat they were generating was bound to combust. Not only his marriage would be ruined, but his career.

Once he told her, she appeared pensive. "How are you certain they will offer such a position?" asked Madlenka, wrapping her words in that accent Stamford found in varying degrees confounding and sexy.

"There's a guy who apparently really has it in for the place, so much so that he's remained on the board looking for an opportunity to derail their mission. Nobody there knows he's come over to our side."

"And you say there are not many who are Black in this institution?"

"That's the other thing. They're supposedly committed to diversity, but they've never walked the walk. This guy, Coyne is his name, says if they put a candidate of color forward, it will call their bluff, and I'll be certain of getting in. All the way around, it's just too good an opportunity to pass up."

Madlenka smiled. "So, you will be playing the race card?"

Stamford knew she was teasing, but a cloud crossed his face. "Let me tell you about the race card, Maddy. The race card in this country is just a Black person getting what's rightfully theirs."

"What is the name of this college?"

"Parana, or something like that."

"Parami?"

"You've heard of it?"

"Pearl Handling, Wyoming. I looked at one of their online certificate programs. Then I decided it was impractical to learn massage therapy from a distance. In certain circles, Parami has an excellent reputation."

"What circles are those?"

"You know. What they used to call the New Age." Madlenka looked away. When she turned back her eyes were glistening. "So, it will be different now."

Stamford nodded.

"This chapter will close?"

He felt like taking her hand, then reminded himself they were in public. "I'm afraid so."

Madlenka shook her head as though some unwanted force was tormenting her. Then calm appeared to settle over her and she took a sip of tea.

"I will be coming with you," she told him.

CHAPTER 6

A Near-Life Experience

Aaron was in a tiny boat, more like a life raft, in the middle of a lake. It was night, and there were no waves, no wind or weather. No oars, no way of propelling himself, but it didn't matter, since he had no strength.

The lake was not large. If he looked left or right, there was darkness, although he sensed a shore on either side. Ahead were dim lights, some sense of inhabitance, and vague activity. With difficulty and strain, he turned to look behind, and it was very much the same, a few distant lights here and there.

Aaron closed his eyes. When they opened seconds or moments or hours later, he felt the mass of his body, his right arm hooked up to a machine. He was in the hospital, he realized, and things started coming back. He'd been in an accident. Someone had stepped on his neck and shoulder. He'd been brought here in an ambulance. He remembered the stars appearing, then dotting out, remembered being out of his body. He'd been back in his body when the attendants wheeled him into a tight, featureless room, had lain there quite a while, a male nurse beside the stretcher, watching over him.

Somehow, at some point, he'd seeped out of his body again, his spirit or mind, whatever it was, configured sideways as it floated from the room. He needed help or he was going to die, and he didn't want to die—he had decided that while confronting the sky and the vanishing stars.

In the hall, he'd righted himself. Several feet away, two doctors stood facing each other, both young, one male, one female. The man was named McDuff, the woman, Powell, although Aaron didn't know how he knew that.

McDuff's face was drawn tight as Aaron heard him say, "Look, I've been here since ten in the morning, and I need to get home."

"There's something seriously wrong with the guy, Mac. His vitals are all over the place. We might even lose him if we don't figure out what's going on, right now, this minute."

McDuff looked at her. "Aren't you sick of it, Jenna?"

Now her face was tight. "Sick of what?"

"All these losers. This endless parade of drunks and druggies, the dregs who think they can coast through life on everybody else's virtue. I'm beginning to ask myself, what do we owe them, do they even deserve to be treated?"

As Doctor Powell looked at her colleague, Aaron felt like grabbing her by the elbow and guiding her into the room where he assumed his body was still prone on the stretcher.

"Are you going back in there to help me find out what's going on with this guy?" she asked.

"I'm going home."

McDuff turned one way and Powell the other as Aaron floated on ahead of her, painfully settling back into his body by the time she got there.

DODIE TEXTED AND called after their unsuccessful attempt at dinner and, when Aaron did not immediately respond, her messages grew increasingly fervent. He finally texted, telling her he'd been in an accident. She sent flowers but didn't come to the hospital. Aaron was disappointed, largely because his condition was making him aware of how alone he was. Many acquaintances but few real friends, none of whom lived in Los Angeles. He found himself thinking a lot about his mother, many years departed. Her family, outside of Detroit, did not approve of her career choice as a band singer. Aaron's father, a trombone player, impregnated her, made Aaron legit at city hall, then split for parts unknown.

Joanne, although those close to her called her Jo, raised Aaron on her own as she toiled for a couple decades as a bookkeeper at a downtown hotel. She smoked sixty Newports a day and drank a fifth of Beefeater's each night, which ultimately reduced her allotted stay on earth. While she drank and smoked she'd listen to Basie, Ellington, Woody Herman, and Maynard Ferguson on her Pioneer stereo.

Aaron shared her love for music, although he never took up an instrument. Especially not the fucking trombone.

With the doctors telling him he was looking at months of rehab, Aaron knew he'd be going it alone. He'd never been close to marrying, had no urge to raise children, yet the words "in sickness and in health" were taking on resonance. It's a bitch to get sick, he told himself, but really a bitch to be sick on your own.

A letter arrived, delivered by one of the nurses.

> Dearest Motherway,
>
> I didn't forget our dinner date that night. I was ardently look-ing forward to seeing you. What happened is, I went for a Sunday afternoon stroll on Venice Beach, and who should I run into but my ex. I hadn't seen him since we sat in some Century City office and signed the divorce papers. I don't regret getting divorced, it's just … he and I, once the process got started, never really got to work it out as people, you know what I mean? We ended up get-ting fish and chips on the pier that Sunday (something we used

to do), and he drove me back to my place, and ... I never dreamed he'd still be there when you showed up.

In a perfect world, I hope you and I can part as friends or at least fond acquaintances. Seeing you in the near future will be challenging since, as I'm sure you've surmised by now, Roger (my ex, current, whatever we are to each other) and I are trying to repair our ruptured union.

Luck to you, Motherway,

Dodie

THROUGHOUT AARON'S FIRST days in the hospital, he slept through the daylight hours, grateful for his morphine drip. The experience of coming out of and then back into his body had replayed. Upon waking, his mind, his spirit, would, more often than not, seep out sideways, then right itself and be there in the room, looking down at his physical form. At first disturbing, he eventually determined that this was a settling, a carryover from his decision, and it was a decision, to not die but to continue living. But, up to this point, what did that life add up to?

Very early on, before his teenage years even, he'd arrived at a cynicism far out of balance with what he'd experienced. That condition, and that is surely what it became, caused him to judge everything that came into his field, dismissing much of it at useless, needless, an absurd distraction. This started internally but eventually manifested as sarcasm, which he now fully recognized as a crude attempt to keep the world at bay. While others were interested in him perhaps, they were too wary to come close. He fashioned himself a romantic, but his interactions skimmed the surface, and what should have been intimate relationships were, on his part anyway, capricious, each with its own predictable conclusion. He'd never adopted any rules, just played an ever-unfolding improvisation, not making things happen but allowing everything, bad and not quite as bad, to happen to him. Now, having encountered a precipice, and declaring he wanted to go on living, he knew he'd need a drastic change in direction and circumstance in order to find an opportunity to give something back to a world with which he'd been, for years, not substantially engaged.

CHAPTER 7

National Search

There were two decent hotels in Pearl Handle. The Queen of the West was old and stately. The Hotel Raphael was on the opposite side of the Middle Street pedestrian mall, and this was the one Daniel Coyne, as head of Parami's Presider Search Committee, selected for Stamford Moses. Besides being newer and shinier, the Raphael was where Daniel stayed after his split with Regina, its efficiency a kind of salve during those disastrous weeks.

Daniel had, for some time, been living in a featureless condo, closer to work, while Regina occupied the house. Pristley appeared to have moved in, leaving his little hovel near the Parami campus largely unoccupied. The divorce wasn't final, but Daniel held no hope of ever getting back with Regina. At least with the success of Agra-gen, he would be coming out of the marriage with money of his own.

Daniel glimpsed his wife and Pristley one evening at Whole Foods. Besides that, the only time he'd see, but not interact with, Regina, was at Parami board meetings. Roger Bayne Whitney convinced Daniel to remain among the Timmons Trustees and offer to steward the Presider search. Regina recused herself from participating in it, clearly wanting as little contact with Daniel as possible.

Daniel had apprised Moses that the search would be swift and crowded, the itinerary resembling a political candidate running for national office. There'd be a Thursday morning trustee breakfast at departing Presider Terence Dillard's Parami-owned residence. The afternoon would be a meeting with selected preceptors, Parami's term for faculty members. Thursday night, a dinner with the Timmons Trustees as well as the Chamber of Wisdom, made up of Parami's highest ranking preceptors and administrators. Friday morning, coffee and croissants with selected junior and senior students, leading up to Friday afternoon's lunch, followed by a final meeting with the trustees, who would convene separately on Friday evening. Formalities concluded, Moses would leave on Saturday, having been selected as Parami University's new Presider.

The Timmons Trustees, some of whom came from other parts of the country as well as Canada and the Virgin Islands, had been in Pearl Handle since Monday. Tuesday and Wednesday, they had put the other finalist, Doctor Norman Rappaport, through similar paces. Rappaport's interviews and informal interactions went remarkably well. Under the normal course of events, Rappaport would have been a firm contender, but Daniel Coyne was going to brandish his influence to ensure that the Reverend Doctor Stamford Moses would be chosen.

At breakfast at Terence Dillard's house, Moses appeared withdrawn, even sullen, and during his interview with high-ranking preceptors, when asked to capsulize his views on Mindfulness Practice, "All my practice is mindful," was all he had to offer.

Before the final meeting with the Timmons Trustees, Daniel noted that Moses had ducked into the newly designated All Genders Restroom. After a moment, Daniel stepped inside and said, "Reverend Moses, are you feeling all right?"

Having washed his hands, Moses was looking around haplessly for something to dry them with. "Why are you asking that question?"

"You seem a little off your game."

Moses fluttered his hands at his sides, apparently having given up hope of finding other means to get them dry. "I thought I was coming out here for a meet and greet. I didn't realize I was going to be asked about a lot of things I don't know or care much about."

"Even Parami has to make some attempt at academic protocol. Best practices demand that we post a national search and select you to come and present yourself."

Moses stopped waving his hands. "What kind of an institution has a washroom without paper towels?"

Daniel stepped closer, lowering his voice. "You're coming off like you're tired or pissed off. You're going to make them hand it over to Rappaport by default."

"Are you telling me I'm not going to be offered the position?"

"I made sure you'd be going up against a white male, so that all you'd have to do for these smug pseudo-liberals is show up and shake hands and tell everyone how excited you are for the future of Parami. But you're not doing that. You're acting like somebody who's been hauled down to the precinct for questioning."

Before responding, Moses glared at Daniel, both of them aware of the indelicate nature of that statement. "You think it's easy to sit in a room with a strangers and have to respond to a bunch of jargon and arcane terminology?"

"I've cleared a path for you. You're going to have to show them something or you're going to blow it." Looking intently at Moses, Daniel added, "Don't forget what this is about. There's a hell of a lot at stake here, reverend."

IN THE TIMMONS Conference Room, Daniel addressed those seated around the massive oak table. "We have time for some questions from individual trustees. Grayson, would you like to start?"

Grayson Keylock rearranged his considerable bulk in the chair, then leaned forward. "Doctor Moses, it's a privilege to have the opportunity to address you directly." He glanced down at his notes. "In your experience in higher education, was there ever a time when you had to think outside the box?"

A look clouded Moses's face. *Think outside the box?* The idiot was asking him to conjure up a nuance out of a cliche. The candidate forced a smile. "Might you be more specific?"

"Give us an example of a time when you had to come up with what you considered to be a wholly unique solution to a problem."

Moses glanced at Daniel, then returned his gaze to his questioner. "There was a time at Greensboro when the annual musical was going to be *The Sound of Music*. We had just one student of color, Dionde Parker was his name, enrolled in the drama department. The young man felt, and I agreed, that there was no role in that play for an African American. He was a great singer, Dionde, had been in church choirs all his life. I urged him to put on a one-man performance featuring inspirational songs by Andraé Crouch and the Reverend James Cleveland. He did so, and it was a rousing success."

Trustee Edith Bonwit leaned forward. "I detect a very faint accent, Reverend Doctor. Were you born in the U.S.?"

"The Bahamas," Stamford replied. "But raised in the South. Florida, to be specific."

"Those performers you just mentioned, I'm not familiar with their work."

"Andraé Crouch? Reverend Cleveland? Amazing singers, both of them."

She smiled tightly. "*Gospel* singers?"

"They would be, yes."

"Which leads us to another question," said Clive Barton, who'd come down from Toronto. "Our founder Lawrence Timmons's philosophy is firmly rooted in Eastern traditions. *Sangha* is what we refer to here as one's community. How much of your own belief system is going to be a fit for the university as you perform your duties?"

Moses smiled tightly. "I think you'll find that the tradition I've been educated in has plenty in common with other, uh, systems of thought. There is divinity in all of us, love thy neighbor, do unto others, and so on. That's all pretty universal, wouldn't you agree?"

Several pairs of eyes darted to various points around the table. Then Grayson Keylock said: "You brought up race earlier in your example about the Black African American boy who felt marginalized during that *Sound of Music* production. Was there ever an instance in your career when you yourself felt discriminated against?"

Reverend Doctor Stamford Moses's hands were on the table, fingers entwined. His shoulder lifted slightly as he drew a breath. Before he could put that breath to use, Daniel Coyne's voice cut through: "I'd like to jump in here."

All eyes went to Daniel, sitting high in his chair. "It's unfortunately clear to me that Doctor Moses is being discriminated against at this very moment."

All at the table except for the candidate turned in his direction.

"Nobody asked Doctor Rappaport if he'd ever been singled out or discriminated against. And why was that? I'll tell you why." Daniel, out of his chair. "Because this is an all-white gathering, posing questions to a candidate of color, questions emanating from their own privileged and entitled experience."

"I resent that implication," said Keylock, all but rising himself. "There's no prejudice here. That is not what this is about. That is not what *Parami* is about."

At the door now, Daniel's eyes swept the room. "As head of this sham committee, I'll allow you to conduct your little inquisition so that you can go ahead and hire someone you're comfortable with, someone in our own image and likeness who'll go on enabling this institution's self-satisfied illusion that we're open and enlightened."

"Now wait a minute, Daniel," said Clive Barton. "What you're saying is a bit harsh. Accusatory, even."

Edith Bonwit rose from the table and stepped over to where Daniel was standing, a quiver in her voice. "The question I asked about gospel singing came from my own unawareness of otherness." She looked at Doctor Moses. "And I apologize for that." She added, "I'm sure those singers are marvelous, Doctor Moses. I intend to listen to some of their recordings as soon as I can find them. Are they on iTunes or Spotify?"

The candidate sat stonelike.

Daniel yanked open the door, then plunged forward, slamming it behind him.

There was a moment of heavy air and averted glances as Moses gathered his composure and stood. "Thank you for this opportunity, gentlemen and gentlewomen. I'll be awaiting your decision."

CHAPTER 8

One Bad Apple

After Aaron was released from the hospital, his injuries, besides the limitations they imposed, triggered a depression, the severity of which he'd never experienced. He had long been accused of being melancholy but now felt he was wearing some borrowed ill-fitting overcoat.

He was looking at months of physical recovery. He set about getting his insurance to settle his hospital expenses and pay for his therapy and car repairs. Several days into this, he was on the phone with a male voice from the automotive division.

"I was paying for uninsured driver coverage," Aaron told him. "You're telling me you aren't covering that?"

"The other party left the scene."

"Right, because he was an uninsured driver."

"That hasn't been substantiated. And besides, you were at fault."

"I wasn't," sputtered Aaron. "The guy plowed through the stop sign. I don't think he even had his lights on."

"That doesn't reflect the police report. Let's see, I have it right here . . . "

Aaron waited, half-listening as the muted voice droned on.

" . . . open container in the car."

"What? That can't be the right report." Then he remembered the wine he'd brought to Dodie's that night. "That container was only open because the bottle smashed on impact."

". . . officer on the scene reported you reeked of alcohol. He couldn't administer a sobriety test because you couldn't walk."

Aaron was speechless.

"There's a strong bias in LA concerning alcohol-related accidents. If you file a claim, you'll likely be going up against law enforcement, the courts. If I were you, I wouldn't like my chances trying to fight that one."

Aaron was told his medical coverage was also being denied for "wanton abuse of a substance resulting in self-induced catastrophe."

His melancholy deepening, he spent most days looking at television or streaming movies. Even with so many options, there was scarcely anything he wanted to watch. He began going to the library, a branch a few blocks away. He revisited books that meant something to him as a young reader. Then he tackled the biggies: *Finnegan's Wake, War and Peace,* all seven volumes of *Remembrance of Things Past.* Each of these works he'd taken up as an undergrad but hadn't finished. This time he read them through.

Days went by with Aaron barely talking with anyone. He felt he was in a kind of quicksand, then realized the analogy wasn't quite right. With quicksand you're sinking, but he felt merely stuck. Okay, in some ways he was sinking. He wasn't making any money, was depleting his savings, and *bankruptcy* had floated through his mind more than once. He'd done nothing but write for a living, and writing seemed like an instrument he'd once played but hadn't picked up in years. He no longer had a screenplay agent, didn't have the energy to go looking for one. His book agent, the one who'd placed *The Sell Out,* had long since stopped calling, then stopped calling back. Aaron couldn't blame her. Failure has a sound as well as a scent and, in their infrequent phone calls, she knew a loser when she heard it.

The only good thing: Aaron's body was healing, although his left side, from his shoulder down to his hand, would likely be a permanent source of discomfort. He'd joined the Y and kept up his physical therapy on the treadmill and with free weights. In a city not known for walking, he walked at least five times a week along the paths in Griffith Park.

One afternoon, his cell phone chimed.

"Is this Aaron Motherway?" a woman asked.

"Yes."

"Aaron Motherway, the author?"

A moment. "Yes."

"Please hold for Doctor Dillard."

Aaron's mind tumbled. The only Doctor Dillard he'd ever known had been his faculty advisor at Michigan State, Doctor Terence Dillard. Must be a mix-up, a misunderstanding. A click and then: "My wife and I loved your book, Aaron."

"Well, thank you."

"You remember me, don't you? Terry Dillard from back at MSU. I'm Presider—president, that is—of Parami University . . . Haven't heard of us? Look on the web, we're unique and highly thought of . . . As I said, Peach—that's my wife—and I loved *Selling Out*. Couldn't stop talking about it."

"Thank you, sir."

"We have an extremely prestigious Arts Program and just had a cancellation for what we call our Summer Passage. I know it's short notice, but might you consider coming out for two weeks and teaching a writing class?"

Aaron thought. "I've never taught before."

Dillard's laugh was loose and warm. "That's okay. Most of our writing instructors have never written a book."

THE CALL FROM Terence Dillard provided Aaron with a purpose, thrusting him into motion. He went online and informed himself about Parami and its founder.

Lawrence Timmons left Columbia in 1969 under a cloud of controversy. He'd been born in 1933 and, until the mid-1960s, was on the traditional trajectory of an academic. Twice married and twice divorced, he had no children. In 1965, a guest lecturer from Berkeley dosed him with lysergic acid diethylamide and Timmons's life changed. The hair got shaggy, then shaggier; the neckties disappeared, as did the Brooks Brothers suits. Within a year he was unrecognizable to colleagues, conducting classes in slack-hanging, self-designed gowns. The population of disaffected students, and there were more of them with each year of that tumultuous decade, would flock to Timmons's townhouse for tea and vegetarian dinners and listening parties featuring the latest vinyl-pressed pronouncements from emerging rock bands.

Besides those gatherings, Timmons oversaw covert midnight wrestling parties, participated in and watched by a select group of exclusively male students. When a seventeen-year-old freshman fractured his femur during one of the bouts, word got out, and the boy's father, a Columbia alum and owner of the most lucrative textile manufacturing company in the Northeast, called for Timmons's termination. The university granted the professor a leave of absence during which the remote possibility of his reinstatement would be determined.

Timmons left the United States with no plan other than to go to the Himalayas to address the unformulated questions swirling within him. The trip was not a smooth one. Timmons, for all his denunciations of material goods, had grown accustomed to regular meals and domestic comforts, none of which were assured in his remote travels. Once, he was set upon by bandits and clubbed with the butt of a rifle. Another time, he got lost in the foothills only to be rescued by a jeep whose driver stopped at the first clearing that resembled a road and mutely pointed, before shoving Timmons out, then speeding away.

The Western professor trudged off in the indicated direction and, after a few miles, came upon a village where some sort of ceremony was taking place, part somber and part almost festive. At one end of the only street, a crowd of elders were assembled, silently watching a body on a gurney being consumed by flames. At the opposite end of the street was a massive pile of garments, all colors and variations of fabric, overseen by a throng of children.

A woman came up beside Timmons and addressed him, surprisingly in English.

What the English-speaking woman told Timmons was that the High Lama of the village and region had dropped his body. He'd been quite old, surely more than a hundred, and ready for his next phase. Now his spirit would guide one of the children to the pile of clothing and that child would extract the one and only garment once belonging to the former guru. Timmons stood near the pile and watched as the assembled children stood immobile.

When the flames from the opposite end of the street subsided, a boy who looked to be four or five moved forward, stepped into the mound of garments, discarding one, then the next, until he came to a peach-shaded sari with gold sequins adorning it. Emerging from the pile, he wrapped it around his tiny frame. All present fell to their knees, chanting the boy's name, "Chodak, Chodak, Chodak!" A wind instrument sounded, bells chimed, and joyous tears were shed.

Timmons remained in the village a couple of days, then was overcome with the sense that he needed to get back to the States and write about his trip, having experienced what he felt to be a sip of enlightenment.

With the success of *This Is Now Here,* published by an underground press and selling an astounding quarter of a million copies, Timmons lectured on campuses and guested on television and radio, dressed much the way he was when jettisoned from Columbia. If, as he surmised, all wisdom was inside, he felt his own was as valid as any guru's from the East.

Not all were enchanted. One reviewer pointed out that *This Is Now Here,* with the last two words combined, spelled *This Is Nowhere.*

Aaron thought about all this and more, driving through the desert past hundred-degree Las Vegas, through Zion National Park, over Vail Pass. He was excited at the prospect of teaching. His own student career had been decidedly undistinguished; attendance spotty, assignments tossed off at the last minute, often submitted late or not turned in at all. He'd only gotten into grad school because of a play he'd written whose student production won the Rita Rourke Award, she being a Michigan State alum who went on to be a widely produced playwright.

With his renewed, post-accident perspective, he would not let these students make the mistakes he'd made. Short term though it was, they'd show up to sessions on time, work in hand, ready to actively participate. He'd give them everything he had, and his effect on them would be lasting.

As Aaron pulled into Pearl Handle at the end of the day on Friday, he was eating an apple. His accommodations were near the Parami campus, but he was in no hurry to get there, figuring to drive around town, check in around six, bump into some dinner, float into a bar.

Gliding through a residential neighborhood, he stopped at an intersection. The AC activated, he pressed the button, rolling down his rented Malibu's automatic window, then tossed the apple core toward the curb, watching it land at the base of a tree. He sent the window back up, continued a couple blocks, then took a left, his instincts telling him he was headed toward the center of town.

At another intersection, he became aware of a dark mass crowding behind him. A woman was at the wheel, glaring, mouth working in what appeared to be intense disapproval. Couldn't be about me, Aaron thought, as he eased across the intersection.

Three blocks later, another intersection, and he was about to turn left when the moss-green, military-type Humvee swung around in front of him, rocking in response to being thrust into park. Aaron watched as the woman lunged from the vehicle and stormed over. No mistaking it, she had murder on her mind, and it somehow involved him. He hit the button, opening the window.

"You've got a lot of nerve, asshole, coming here and defacing my town."

Aaron got a better look at her; brunette mane, silver racing stripe sweeping back from her forehead, all the way across her crown. Her face gone scarlet, a prominent vein, thick as an earthworm, was pulsing inside her forehead. She was around sixty, and a coronary did not seem out of the question. "What are you talking about?" he asked.

"That APPLE CORE. You tossed it like a used Kleenex after fucking somebody. Go back there and pick it up."

Aaron held his smile, kept his voice low and even. "It's ah, biodegradable, you know. Don't you think the birds will eat it?"

Her face twisted. Aaron felt she was an increment away from springing forward, nails and teeth bared. "YOU EAT IT, MISTER! EAT IT, YOU SELFISH, ARROGANT, ENTITLED ASSHOLE! YOU AND YOUR LAME-ASSED CALIFORNIA LICENSE PLATES!"

Aaron pressed the button, closing the window. She was still in the intersection flailing and shouting as he eased around her tank of a car, then pulled away.

CHAPTER 9

Summer Passage

In 1995, Parami purchased an abandoned hospital on Many Whips Avenue whose grounds became the central official campus. Now all that remained of the hospital was Timmons Hall, which housed the President's office, the Plateau Performance Space, and several other offices and classrooms. Adjacent to these was a narrow, dilapidated bell tower with a gigantic bell whose clapper had been removed a few decades before.

The hospital had come with substantial grounds, and Parami constructed an array of yurts and domes and huts where classes were held, along with weather-worn cottages that served as preceptor offices. There was the two-story yellow-brick Timmons Library, above which was a slew of administrative offices, such as Admissions, the Registrar, Student Services, Inclusion and Diversity, Sustainability, and Sentient Resources. Academic Engagement had its own bungalow on the northernmost edge of the campus. Parami also had satellite offices and classrooms at four other locations in Pearl Handle. What Parami did not have was a student union, a rec center, a bookstore, or dormitories. Students were expected to find housing and fend for themselves.

Although Aaron would be teaching only two weeks, ten sessions in all, he drastically over-prepared. Summer Passage differed from the year-round program in that students could take classes for credit or non-credit. Aaron titled his course The Art of Adaptation: What to Show and What Not to Tell, figuring he could apply his renewed literary thirst as well as his experience as a scriptwright. To devise a course description, he'd consulted a couple of previous summer catalogs, posted online.

B. H. Everett, a language poet from Brattleboro, Vermont, offered the following:

> **COMMUNING WITH THE SHADOW SELF:** We will spend the first week in outdoor discussion, holding in our consciousness the awareness that we are constantly casting a shadow. For Week Two, some will compose siren songs (not vocalized but in text) to entice their shadow back into their being. Others may choose to stomp on their shadow, emitting primal, nonverbal incantations, sending that wounded and indistinct part of them back into the earth.

Aaron simply stated what he intended to do as clearly and straight-forwardly as he could, hoping that enough students would sign up for the class to run. When he received the class roster via email, he was delighted that ten students—which struck him as a highly respectable number—had registered, just two below the maximum.

The night before class, in his queen-size bed in the Golden Bison Motor Lodge, Aaron awoke in a panic. He'd written for the screen and had written a novel but was overcome with the sense that he had no prac-tical wisdom to offer to any prospective writer. "Just sit your butt down in a chair and don't get distracted," was as much as he had.

After an essentially sleepless night, Aaron watched the dark turn to dawn, then strolled along Sycamore Boulevard and discovered an hon-est-to-God diner. During a suitably greasy breakfast, he read the hot-off-the-press *Recorder*, then walked the streets of Pearl Handle, vaguely considering a drive back to Los Angeles, when he realized he was several blocks from Parami and would need to hustle to not be late for his nine o'clock class.

When he got there at two minutes before nine, he was surprised to see a mere three students in attendance. Before even introducing himself, what slipped out of Aaron's mouth was the pathetic utterance: "Where is everybody?"

A young woman wearing a Lou Reed *Rock 'n' Roll Animal* T-shirt said: "Welcome to Parami, man."

Trying not to seem flustered, Aaron set about taking attendance. Two names in, a scrawny but muscled guy who was aiming at some ironic version of skinhead, accompanied by a woman in her forties who looked like a small-town librarian, breezed in together. Aaron didn't react, other than clumsily establishing that they were indeed signed up for the course.

"My name is Aaron Motherway, and I've never done this before."

"Done what, dude?" the faux skinhead said, and everyone but Aaron laughed.

Aaron paused, then said, "You're all writers, correct?"

"We want to be," said the Lou Reed fan.

"So, this class is about adaptation. Definitely part of the job description. Even if you want to write novels and have no interest in writing for the screen, it's something you should become acquainted with because it's all about narrative structure, looking at a work of literature and determining how to present it dramatically. Even though you're working with preexisting material, it's inherently creative and anything but straightforward."

Three young men came in, two with backward ball caps, the other with golden dreads. As they noisily found seats, Aaron didn't feel like establishing who they were, but simply pressed forward. "How many times have you read a book, then gone to see the film only to be disappointed?"

A long-haired young woman traipsed in, cell phone to her ear. As she scanned the room for a seat, she was saying, "Oh, Bonnie, you're awesome. Stick a pin in this and I'll call you later. Class is about to start."

As she passed in front of Aaron, he caught a gag-inducing whiff of chemicals, giving him the impression that the young woman had spent the moments just before, coloring her nails outside. Aaron tried to reset, in order to continue, but his brain sputtered. When his lips moved, his head turned, and he heard himself say to the young woman, "Why are you late?"

She looked at him, eyelashes blinking as though she'd wandered into a dust storm. Aaron sensed that everyone in the room was sitting up a little higher.

More blinks from the young woman, then Aaron said, "Just find a seat, please." He shifted gears once more. "About adaptation. Let's look at an example. *The Great Gatsby*, we all know it—read it in high school, saw the movie—starts with Nick Carraway talking about his father and the family drugstore back in Minnesota and his great-uncle sending a substitute to fight in the Civil War. If you're adapting that material, are you going to put all those details up on the screen? No, the story, the dramatic action, begins with Nick going across the bay to have dinner with his cousin Daisy and her husband, Tom Buchanan."

A young man wearing tattered jeans, Converse high-tops and Ray-Bans ambled in. Aaron glanced at his watch. Nine twenty-two. Aaron stared at the young man who was scanning the room for a seat. The odor of nail polish was now mingled with the smell of cannabis, an invisible cloud surrounding the young man's head and shoulders.

"And why are *you* late?" asked Aaron.

The guy smiled. "What?"

"You kept us waiting. Why?"

The young man shook his head as though to clear it. "My roommate forgot to set the alarm."

Aaron shook his head. "No, that's not the reason."

The guy grinned and turned to the class as though seeking support, all of them simply staring at him. "Well, there was a lot of traffic . . . and there's construction on Fifteenth."

Again, Aaron shook his head. "No, that's not it either."

The guy was smiling but it was a tight smile, the veins in his neck pulsating. "Okay, bro, I give up. Why don't you tell me?"

Aaron drew a breath. "The secret to getting to a place on time is to leave the place you're starting from with enough time to get to where you're going." Now Aaron felt himself involuntarily moving toward the door. "All any of us have in this life is our time. And with only a few exceptions, you just wasted some of mine." At the door. "Tomorrow morning, at nine o'clock sharp, I'll be closing the door. If you show up here and the door is closed, don't come in, because you won't be welcome." He turned and looked at them. "Even though you're paying for this class, it doesn't mean you're buying it. I'll see you, those of you who want to participate, at nine tomorrow morning. Those of you who can't make it then, I suggest you go to the Summer Passage office and find another workshop."

Aaron stepped outside, slamming the door behind him.

BACK AT THE Golden Bison, Aaron stayed in bed most of the day, channel changer in hand, watching the satellite-borne images flicker before him. Around six o'clock in the evening, he picked up the set of local menus provided by the motor lodge and ordered basil fried rice from the Bangkok Palace. There were four cans of Dale's Pale Ale in the small icebox; he drank three with dinner, and before he knew it, it was eleven o'clock and neither his room extension nor his cell phone had sounded. He checked his email—nothing from Parami—then fell into a shallow sleep, waking around two and again at five.

At dawn, he trudged into Pearl Handle, which was rustling with joggers, cyclists, and early morning commuters. He had breakfast at the

Enlightened Coffee Shop, which is to say he had coffee and a bran muf-
fin, as baked goods were all that was on the menu. As he sipped and
swallowed, he was serenaded by Miles Davis with notes and intervals
never intended for the light of day.

He got back to the motor lodge a little after eight, rechecked his
phone and computer, then inquired at the desk. No message, nothing.
Aaron figured the Summer Passage office was simply waiting for him to
show his face before informing him that his students had been funneled
into other workshops.

When he got to Parami at ten minutes to nine, Viti Balakrishnan,
the sunny, mid-twenties administrator of the Arts Program, greeted him
by smiling and handing over a fresh set of papers tucked into a clear
plastic binder. Although her heritage emanated from South India, Viti
was born and raised in Fayetteville, Arkansas. With a melodious drawl
she said, "We have a bit of a change, Aaron, that you can say no to if you
want."

"What is it?"

"Some students end up in workshops they don't feel are right for
them, so they request to be moved."

Here it comes. Aaron took the binder from her and glanced down.

"As you know," Viti continued, "we cap our classes at twelve, but
whatever you covered yesterday, word got out, and you have seven more
students wanting to take your workshop. You can say no to adding any
students, or you can just admit a couple or a few, but if you have more
than twelve, we'll need to move you to a bigger classroom."

Aaron silently counted as he scanned the list. *Seventeen students.*
"Nobody dropped?"

"Not one. Why?"

"Just . . . you never know how the first day is going to go."

"So, what do you say?"

Aaron thought a moment. "I'll accept whoever wants to take the
class."

"Great. Why don't you relax while I go over and get everyone set-tled into the new space. Help yourself to that little spread in the corner. There's chai and gluten-free donuts."

Aaron passed on the food offer, just sat and thumbed through a copy of the current Summer Passage catalog.

> TAGGING THE DOMINANT CULTURE: We will venture out into the community and identify urban surfaces upon which we might, given the opportunity of darkness and anonymity, scrawl provocative, even incendiary three-word poems. Please note: this venture is conceptual in nature and is not designed to put you or your classmates in danger of arrest or confinement.

"Aaron, they're ready for you."

Roster in hand, Aaron was led by Viti to Timmons Studio on the first floor of Timmons Hall. Aaron immediately noted that the rooms appeared more spacious and functional than the others on campus.

As he walked into the classroom, he recognized a few faces, aware that several others had not been present the day before. Everyone appeared to be sitting high in their seats and all eyes were on him. He strode to the desk, dropped the roster on top of it, and faced the class. "As I was saying . . ."

CHAPTER 10

Bird Blew Alto

Summer Passage offered its participants—students and preceptors—total immersion, and during that first week, Aaron was totally immersed. Besides his morning workshop, there were panels and lectures throughout the afternoon and a full slate of readings in the evening.

Each event was recorded, visually and in sound, for the Parami Arts Repository. This practice had been inaugurated by the late Willard Pettibone, Arts Program founder and infamous hoarder. He felt that Parami represented a true and viable cultural alternative, and the work and perspectives of the participants must be documented. Trouble was, by assiduously recording all the proceedings of the Arts Program, no one ever properly assumed the task of organizing the thousands of hours of recorded material, so they languished in a warehouse outside of Pearl Handle, many of the now departed voices lying fallow.

Every few years, some advocate of the Arts Program or some motivated student would make noises about the massive mound of information that needed to be digitized and categorized. But the interested party would then grow discouraged at the Sisyphean nature of the undertaking, and enthusiasm would sputter. At one point early on, the enterprising Pettibone approached a collective of rock bands to jumpstart the project with what for them would be a sizable tax write-off, but nothing seemed to come of it.

On Friday at the end of week one, Aaron attended a lecture in Para-mi's Plateau Performance Space by year-round preceptor Philip Pristley, "Spontaneous Combustion: Process as Destination."

Pristley wore a denim shirt and pants above a pair of well-worn moccasins. Broad shouldered and thick-chested, his legs, by contrast, appeared quite thin. His hair was pulled back into a ponytail, so black it gleamed under the stage lights, and Aaron had the impression that the color might not have been natural. Clearly enamored of his own resonant voice, Pristley crooned into a handheld mic.

"Don't be afraid to fail, because there's no such thing as failure. These false constructs that writers concoct, fiction writers especially, are labored and predictable and repressive and keep what passes as literature with one foot in the nineteenth century. We're talking dead form and dead language, the product of a dying culture."

Aaron took in the crowd of students, a number of whom were duti-fully scribbling in their notebooks. As he listened, a response swirled in him.

Pristley brought the presentation to a close, then set about fielding questions from the audience, softballs lobbed from various young women seated near the front. "I think we have time for one more." Aaron's was the sole hand that went up, practically before he was aware of it. Pristley said, with a trace of reluctance, "Uh, okay, in the back there."

Aaron felt heads turn and sets of eyes train on him like he was in the sights of a massive SWAT team. He rose, and a student techie material-ized, thrusting a mic in Aaron's face. "Rather than an experiment," Aaron said, "wouldn't you prefer to see or read a culmination?"

A thud of silence, then Pristley shook his head. "I'm not following you, man."

"Well, all writing, all art, is an experiment in its early stages, but when it's presented, on the page or in public, shouldn't it be fully realized?

It may not be, but don't you want to feel that the artist considers it as such?"

The stage lights must have been glaring, for Pristley shielded his eyes with one hand as he took a step forward. "You're not a student, are you? You're a guest instructor?"

Aaron didn't know what that had to do with his question, so he didn't respond.

Pristley chuckled. "You must have noticed the title for today's talk, which you obviously don't agree with. And that's fine. We don't all have to be in love with each other. But for the sake of argument—or, you know, discussion—do you consider Gertrude Stein an experimental writer?"

Aaron thought a moment. "She certainly experimented. But what she published was completely cooked."

Pristley nodded pensively. "So, the process, the passage if you will, isn't important to you?"

"Well, sure it is. But when I see a great athlete playing, I don't want to be aware of all those hours they put in at the gym or on the practice field. Don't want their mind involved at all. I just want to see fluid, masterful action."

Pristley smiled. "We don't got no jocks here at Prommy."

Delivered with a shitkicker accent, this got a big laugh, which Pristley clearly relished.

The lights dimmed and came up again, indicating that the lecture was over. But Pristley was on a roll. "Since your example wasn't literary, I guess you'd have Charlie Parker sketch out every note before taking a trumpet solo."

Aaron paused as though about to take a steep dive into a pool whose depth had not been determined. *Fuck it.* "Charlie Parker didn't play the trumpet, my friend. He played sax."

Shadows and silence, along with a few titters. The lights came fully on, and the crowd rose from their respective seats, accompanied by indeterminate clamor. As things kept shifting in the room, Pristley glared at Aaron, then strode off the stage.

The following Monday, for his second week, around half of Aaron's students turned up in gray T-shirts with bright blue letters across the front: *Bird Blew Alto.*

AARON WAS SCHEDULED to leave on Sunday. On Friday he received a message at the Golden Bison from Terence Dillard: *Come to dinner at Presider's house tomorrow evening. Student driver will pick you up at 6:45.*

Aaron was surprised by the invitation. First off, he hadn't caught a glimpse of Parami's Presider since he'd arrived and had been kept too busy to seek him out. Plus, he'd never gotten over the fact that Dillard, someone he figured on never seeing again after leaving East Lansing, was playing any kind of role in his life.

Sunday evening, Aaron was picked up by a twentyish male in an ancient Mercedes. Aaron had noted that all the Parami vehicles were high-end makes—Mercedes, BMW, Lincoln, and Cadillac—but none seemed newer than twenty years old, likely gifts from donors who were no longer on the roll to provide replacements.

The car pulled up in front of a sprawling split-level house on the outskirts of Pearl Handle. No houses on either side, and a significant amount of open space lay behind it. Aaron was greeted at the door by a young female he assumed was another Parami student or employee and ushered into the living room.

Dillard sat in a massive armchair in front of a wide-screen television, a well-fed yellow lab drowsing at his feet. It had been two decades, and the man's hair was grayer, but he wore the same style horn-rimmed glasses and appeared to have not put on a pound. Aaron surely would have recognized him on the street. There were no other guests present. Dillard clicked off the set and stood. "I'm drinking single malt. Care to join me?"

"Sure," said Aaron.

Dillard told the young woman to get Aaron a scotch on the rocks. Once Aaron had settled on the sofa and a flurry of small talk had been dispensed with, Dillard said: "Do you ever think about East Lansing, Aaron?"

"Not too often. You do?"

A curious expression clouded the older man's face. "At least once a day, sometimes more. Some of my best years were spent at MSU. You don't feel that way?"

Aaron took a moment. "Sir, I'm afraid I wasn't very serious at that point of my life."

"Well, you seemed to enjoy yourself."

"I was having a good time, I guess. And I managed to get admitted to grad school. But I was just . . . " Aaron, feeling oddly emotional, felt his voice trail off. "I'm surprised you even considered me to teach this summer."

"Well, you obviously made an impression back then. You were cynical, I recall, more cynical than you had a right to be at that age. But there was something about you that was . . . well, unforgettable." Dillard set his glass on a small end table. "Aaron, I'd like you to come back to Parami this fall and run the Arts Program for us."

Aaron looked at Dillard, his thoughts scrambled. "The Arts Program, run it?"

"You'll be designated as *Seat*, from the Buddhist concept of taking your seat, or assuming your position. You'll be responsible for the entire program and all its concentrations, an interim appointment for the Fall and Spring Passages. But I have no doubt you'll make yourself indispensable. I want someone who will come in and objectively assess things and put their stamp on the program." He looked at him earnestly. "Parami can really use you, Aaron."

Aaron sat, Dillard not taking his eyes off him. "I don't know what to say, Doctor Dillard."

"Don't say anything. Just look over the very straightforward letter of offer I've had Parami's attorneys prepare. Sign it and get it back to me ASAP."

Dillard stood, startling the dog stretched out in front of him. The lab rose clumsily, shook its large head, and let out a half-hearted bark. Dillard laughed. "I'll run upstairs and get Peach and then let's eat, shall we?"

PART TWO
LINGERING

Incoming

The Pickering house, in Peppermill, Virginia, was surrounded by rolling hills and lively fields, eighty acres of breathtaking property. The family had owned it for five years, but for the most part it had gone unoccupied. A couple of Thanksgivings had been celebrated there, and one Christmas, but it had not until recently turned into the alternative residence that Joel and Beverly Pickering had intended when they purchased it.

Joel was as busy as humans can make themselves, being one of the primary estate planners in the United States. When the Obama administration was parceling out assignments for its first term, he'd been short-listed as Secretary of the Treasury but let it be known he wasn't interested. Who needed the immense pay cut and the capriciousness of electoral politics?

The family, the only child being seventeen-year-old Nolan, lived in Georgetown. Yet this past spring, Bev had become infused with a sudden commitment to the Peppermill property, making the two-and-a-half-hour drive three or four times a week to oversee a hastily inducted squad of landscapers, roofers, carpenters, and domestics. Bev delegated tasks like a stage director speeding toward production. This all began toward the end of March, and by Memorial Day, the pool was in, the gardens sculpted, the house freshly painted and furnished. Nolan graduated high school the first week of June. The following week, he and his mother relocated to rural Virginia.

This was a development Nolan was not pleased about. He didn't drive, felt no need to in the District, knew no one in Peppermill County. There was only one restaurant, only one that his mother would go to anyway, and the property, undeniably impressive, soon struck him as desolate.

He couldn't get used to the house. There were seven bedrooms and each—quilted and quaint—seemed barren to him. The house was a chamber of footsteps, voices, the most subtle activity engulfed in reverberation. After nightfall, the hills and fields turned unfriendly, sites for all manner of lurking and intrigue and threat. Nolan kept test-driving various bedrooms, upstairs and down, couldn't get comfortable in any of them. One night he dreamed a company of ragged Confederate soldiers were dragging themselves along the road that ran in front of the house.

His father appeared twice that summer, arriving late on Saturday afternoon and sharing dinner, once at the house, once at the dreaded restaurant, only to rush back to Georgetown, once before noon, once before dawn.

The night in question, the night that changed everything, Nolan was in an upstairs bedroom. Was he awake, asleep, half-asleep? Difficult to say, as his sleep there had grown so restless and disturbed that each night he remained, waking or sleeping, attuned to the house's creaks and rustlings, trying to arrive at a state of dark quietude.

He'd been reading, and the book had tumbled, open and not bookmarked, onto the floor. The title was *What Would You Do If You Knew What to Do?* by Lawrence Timmons, whose writings Nolan had discovered and was clinging to like a lifeline.

There had been talk of his father coming that weekend, but Saturday, when he hadn't arrived by dusk, Nolan and his mother went to the restaurant, then returned home to drift in their respective distractions. He'd turned in, he would recall, around eleven thirty.

In a later statement, Nolan said that after midnight, closer to one, he heard a crack or a pop, and then a sound he'd never heard before, a low gurgling. He made his way cautiously, he said, only to come upon the sight of a figure crawling on the floor of the upstairs hallway. His mother stood in the dim light of the doorway, arm at her side, pistol in hand, a sharp scent in the air that Nolan assumed was gun powder. Before any word was said, Nolan recognized his father, face down, no longer gurgling or moving. Nolan didn't lean over his father's body, he recounted, but looked at his mother, who said: "I thought it was an intruder."

Beverly Pickering spent several hours at the Peppermill County sheriff's department, wisely not saying much until Gil Stottlemeyer, personal counsel to power brokers and presidents, arrived from the District and she was, if not set free, then released from custody. No charges were immediately brought, pending an investigation. Bev later offered some details about an unnerving encounter with an unidentified local man who'd wanted to fish in the pond but had been denied that request by Bev herself. So surly and truculent was he, that she brought out, from Georgetown, a .22 pistol registered to Joel, in case the local man made good on his "I'll be back" statement, which Bev interpreted as a threat.

Stottlemeyer had been unable to locate the person Bev described. The state's attorney found one local who stated in a deposition that yes, he'd come on the property as he'd heard the pond had been freshly stocked, but when Mrs. Pickering informed him that she would not be allowing fishing due to insurance considerations, the man thanked her for her time, climbed into his pickup, and left.

Nolan's only solace through all this was his reading of Lawrence Timmons. Nolan had hoped to go to Sidney where Timmons was living, to study with him directly. Through internet navigations, he found that Timmons, now in his eighties, had taken a vow of silence two years before, removing himself from any but the most cursory human contact. As a kind of consolation, Nolan applied to, and was accepted by, the Timmons-founded Parami University. A big part of him was relieved to be getting away from the tragedy and going off to Wyoming in the fall; a place that, from what he'd seen on various websites, was nothing like gentlemanly Georgetown or haunted, unruly rural Virginia.

OPHELIA JENKS, EIGHTEEN, was in her bedroom in Winnetka, Illinois, staring at the U.S. map on the far wall. It was a new addition to her room, having just been unfolded and tacked up. Reclining on the bed, Ophelia clutched a dart, steel-tipped with a green plastic tail, one of two survivors (the other red) from an ancient set. Ophelia was about to make a big shift in her life, about to determine where she would attend college. Her approach: she'd toss the dart at the map, and wherever it landed, she'd go on the internet, find three institutions in or nearest to that region, then set about the irksome application process.

That she might not be admitted was not a flicker in her mind. What she might study was not a consideration. Ophelia didn't want to go to *any* school, had been unwavering on that conviction throughout her time at New Trier. That's why she'd been free to accompany her parents on the cruise they all took right after graduation, that disastrous cycle of weeks that had landed Ophelia in such foul soup that she found herself in the uncharacteristic predicament of having to do something they wanted her to do.

She was an only child. Adopted. Their home was on Sheridan, iron-gated and sprawling, the back facing Lake Michigan. Ophelia loved it here. Her room. Her red Alfa. Late nights on Hubbard Street flashing her fake ID. Sleeping till one or two. A maid and a cook. The beach just beyond her bedroom window. Why couldn't she just stay here? Why did everything have to change?

"There are certain benchmarks in life," her father had instructed, "certain times to do things, and this is the time for you to get a college education. I don't care where you go. You just need to take that step, Ophelia. It's vital."

Her father was remote but formidable, having been successful as a manufacturer of heavy machinery. Prior to the cruise, she'd held him off about college, claiming she needed a gap year. But the cruise changed everything.

Alone in the ship's dining hall one evening, Ophelia, bored and confined, decided she would have a shipboard affair with the next man who stepped through the door. When it came to males, an age gulf was not out of the realm of Ophelia's experience. She always set her sights on older—sometimes much older—men or younger women.

The men she chose would get obsessed and act foolish. The girls/women would become confused and usually end up never speaking to her again.

With older men, she'd start out innocent, making them feel they were in charge, that it was they who were corrupting her. Then in a car or hotel room or empty office, Ophelia would turn it on in ways most of these men had never known or experienced.

With girls, starting from when she was thirteen, Ophelia would get them to be friends by making up stories she would claim she'd never revealed to anyone—incest, arson, suicide attempts—inducing them in turn to pour out their innermost fears and wants and secrets. Then, at summer camp or during a sleepover, or when parents were away and there was plenty of opportunity, Ophelia would have them.

The nautical episode featured the ship's captain, twenty-six years her senior, who ended up drunk two nights later, taking a dare from Ophelia, which sent him headfirst off the starboard side of the ship while docked in Athens.

There was a twenty-four-hour delay as another captain was dispatched from the line's headquarters. Ophelia and her parents were asked to quit the cruise, which they did, flying home twenty days early. Things had been frosty at the Jenks household ever since the return.

Change was called for, hence Ophelia's unconventional approach to choosing a school. She drew a bead on the colorful map. Closing her eyes, she drew back and released the green plastic missile. It landed true, sticking mid-left. Ophelia bounded from the bed. *Wyoming.* She went to her Mac, glowing on the chaotic surface of the desk, nestled among half-eaten energy bars and Tarot cards and cans of Diet Coke. Activating the search engine, she typed: Wyoming, colleges and universities.

Not many to choose from. Parami came up second, and she was immediately intrigued. A few pithy Willard Pettibone quotes convinced her. It was stated that Parami had "rolling admissions," which meant there was no deadline, and she could apply for the fall, only four weeks away. Neither the SAT nor the ACT were required, and the acceptance rate was a warm and welcoming 98.5%. For the first time in quite a while, she felt excited.

Ophelia Jenks was heading West.

CHAPTER 12

We, The Undersigned

Aaron rented a loft on the other side of Middle Street. Feeling no urge to have a car in Pearl Handle, he walked to Parami on the first day of his contract. He was starting out anew, embarking on a path that could very well occupy him for the rest of his working life. He was delighted to be part of a truly alternative institution. So thorough was his preparation, he'd even read—on the Parami website—all five hundred twenty-six pages of the *Preceptor Compendium*, which served as a faculty handbook. Everything in his life had shifted, owing to Doctor Dillard's astounding and long-held belief. Aaron looked forward to thanking him again.

As with the Summer Passage headquarters, the Arts Program's offices were in Timmons House, a dilapidated two-story structure on the westernmost edge of the campus. A paved drive on one side turned into a cul-de-sac. On the occasions when Aaron had been to the arts offices during the summer, he'd always walked up the drive, then swung right to the back door, as nobody ever seemed to use the front. On this, his first day of officially being in charge, he cut through an untamed patch of earth leading directly to the front entrance, making his way across the irregular terrain. He'd taken about ten steps when he felt his right leg plunge downward, not connecting with solid ground. His body swerved right until at last the bottom of his foot connected with . . . *What?* Something fleshy that squirmed beneath his shoe. He heard a startled and startling cry and felt something swoosh upward along his pant leg. Aaron's body lurched forward, open palms slamming to the ground, protecting his face. When he lifted his head, his eyes caught a glimpse—some object, some moving object—which produced yet another shriek, yelp, some sound, wholly foreign.

A pain shot from Aaron's right ankle to his knee. Hoping to hell nothing was broken, he awkwardly tugged himself up from the hole, his eyes catching several beige blurs, off to the right and much closer in the foreground. He trained his sight on the nearest creature, a plump mass of tan fur. *What the hell? A gopher?* That's what he'd tumbled into, a gopher hole. More movement to the left and in the distance, a dozen scurrying forms bounding in all directions, like so many baked loaves come to life, emitting high-pitched, frantic chattering.

Aaron groaned to his feet. His ankle throbbed but didn't feel shattered. He hoped his neck and shoulder and arm were not newly injured. He moved cautiously toward Timmons House, eyes cast down, as though crossing a minefield. There were several holes before him, each the circumference of a bowling ball.

When he reached the tiny front porch, the door swung open. Viti, so helpful to Aaron all summer, stood wrapped in a colorful sari.

"You fell into one, didn't you?" she said, in her incongruous Dixie accent.

"You saw it?"

"I heard it. The prairie dogs go crazy when somebody does that. I'm so used to the little buggers, I didn't think to warn you."

"Why the hell aren't there signs posted? How many of them are out there?"

"Last I heard, over two hundred."

Aaron followed her into the office. "They're just allowed to live here?"

"There was an attempt a few years ago to displace them, but a number of students protested. I can't stand them myself. They're really nothing but bobtailed rats, and I hear they can carry bubonic plague."

VITI SAT AT a huge ancient desk in what would, in most office configurations, be a receptionist's post. This demanded that she double as first point of contact, both in person and on the phone, as well as navigate through a perpetual blizzard of administrative duties. It was clear to Aaron that Viti held the moving parts of the program together, and he set up his office in the room adjacent to where she sat.

In anticipation of Fall Passage, Aaron had already held a series of phone meetings with Viti to ensure that he, insofar as possible, was brought up to speed. Spread out on the table in the Absorption Room, the least utilized space in Timmons House, were student-generated course evaluations and exit surveys, along with preceptor contracts, promotion materials, and syllabi.

"Our new Presider wants to meet with you today," Viti said, in her tuneful Southern accent. "Seems like he's shaking things up already. I learned this morning he's changing my job title from administrative assistant to Protocol Facilitator."

"New *Presider?*" Aaron uttered. "What about Doctor Dillard?"

"Nobody told you? Dillard retired right after Summer Passage. Reverend Moses just got here from some school in Iowa."

"*Reverend?*"

"Hardly makes sense, but c'mon, Aaron, we got a lot of work to do."

Unsettled, Aaron took a sip of coffee, purchased from the Parami food truck, what the university had to offer in lieu of a café. The coffee, like all other liquid dispensed from the massive, metal-gray vehicle, tasted vaguely of chai. Whatever had gone down, Dillard had brought him here and, as Viti so flatly indicated, there was a hell of a lot of work ahead. "What day of the week have you been holding preceptor meetings?" he asked, setting his cup aside.

Viti gave him a look. "We stopped having them three years ago."

Aaron was puzzled.

"Nobody came regularly," Viti continued, "and when they did, they all just ended up complaining without the faintest inclination to fix anything. Truthfully, Aaron, I'd urge you to not start them up again."

He kept listening.

"There's really no upside. Besides being more work for me, it would give them the opportunity to gang up on you. Divide and conquer is likely your best approach, and they're already in their own separate silos."

"Okay, let's take a look at the arts preceptors. Tell me about Elia Adank."

"From Wisconsin. Met Pettibone in the eighties and Pettibone brought him to Parami. He speaks seven languages and refuses to read or write in English. Try having a conversation, and you'll find he never says anything, just chuckles when he finds something amusing, which is more often than you'd think. And don't bother assigning him to a university committee; he won't have any of it."

"But he's supposed to serve on a committee; it's in the compendium."

"His family is loaded, having invented bratwurst or something. Every year, Elia donates a sum to the university that matches his salary. So, he's essentially working here to give himself something to do."

"Okay, what about Connie Yang? She wasn't around this summer and I don't see her listed as teaching any classes."

"We cover her course load with adjuncts. It's unlikely you'll meet her anytime soon, if ever."

"Why not? She's a preceptor."

"Extended sabbatical. Keeps getting grants to work on The Long March as Long Poem."

"And what exactly is that?"

"Are you aware of Mao Tse-tung's Long March?"

"I don't know, I guess."

"Well, that's the epic Connie's supposedly writing. Her real name is Celeste Howser. Note that there's no photo accompanying her bio. She's as white as Taylor Swift but her maternal grandmother's second husband was Chinese, and she's assumed his name to keep snagging multicultural project grants, although the jury's out as to whether she'll ever finish."

"Why wouldn't she, if she gets all that support?"

Viti smiled. "The Long March itself took ten years and so far, Connie's been at it eleven."

"What about Philip Pristley, and why do we have a *guy* teaching Feminist Theory?"

Viti reached over and pushed some fresh documents toward Aaron with a wan smile. "I wasn't sure I was going to show you this."

Aaron looked down at the top sheet:

> *We, the undersigned students of Parami University's Arts Program, do hereby formally and vigorously protest the appointment of one Aaron Motherway as Interim Seat. Motherway's sole published work is more in keeping with his commerce-ridden Hollywood background and, in public discussions during Summer Passage, has shown himself to be an unsuitable fit regarding Parami's alternative aesthetic.*

There followed a page and a half of signatures. Aaron felt heat rising on the back of his neck.

"Philip was Seat the last seven years, although he never had to do much, never even moved into this office. You will be pleased to hear," added Viti, "that several students refused to sign, every one of them from your workshop over the summer."

"You're telling me Pristley is behind this?"

"He had his minions circulate it after it was announced you'd been appointed."

Now the heat was edging toward the top of Aaron's skull. Everything else on the table would have to wait. "Well, that's a shot across the bow. Tell me everything you know about him."

CHAPTER 13

Taking Your Seat

To trace Philip Pristley's trajectory at Parami, one had to start with Axis, the first Archon (director) of the Arts Program's Performance Focus.

Her surname was Coogan and her given name Evelyn, but she'd called herself Axis ever since the launch of her public life, which commenced early. She had an inside track, being the youngest and most favored sibling of Guy Coogan, founder and curator of Lakshmi, generally assumed to be the hippest-ever gallery in London.

Axis grew up with rock royalty, film stars, and their even-more-celebrated directors; painters too, of course; and writers and photographers and designers and supermodels. By age twenty, she was consumed with ambition if only she could light upon a career. "Just pick something," her brother told her. "Anything; I know everybody worth knowing, and I'll make it happen."

During the latter days of punk, Axis became a musician. That is, she donned a beat-to-shit Fender Mustang and was considered a musician as she ranted and strutted before an ever-changing assemblage of The Celestial Slugs, a perennially dopesick backing unit, who produced the sonic landscape for which Axis assumed, on her brother's ardent counsel, sole songwriting and publishing credit. Her much-celebrated lyrics were cut-ups inspired by the collaborations of Brion Gysin and William S. Burroughs in which they would shred texts, then reconfigure all the elements in random order. Axis's most celebrated song, "Bolshevik Conjunctions," was appropriated from page 280 of a translation she owned but had never read of *Notes from the Underground*.

Having taken ecstasy while playing at a reunion concert at the Royal Albert Hall, Axis experienced her spirit leaving her body and settling into one of the balcony seats. She turned to her right, saw herself in the seat next to her and heard that version of herself remark: "A bit off tonight, don't you think, luv?"

Axis didn't know how she finished the set, and at a continuation of the tour the next night in Glasgow, she froze up and couldn't go on. This precipitated a breakdown, and, for nearly two years, she did little besides eat, sleep, and subject herself to endless viewings of *Cocktail*, a second-shelf Hollywood offering starring Tom Cruise and Elizabeth Shue. Axis's family was more than a little concerned. Finally, globe-hopping Willard Pettibone, longtime family friend and occasional lover of brother Guy, appeared at Axis's bedside, shortly after Parami's Arts Program had evolved from a nonaccredited summer festival to a year-round, fully accredited, albeit loosely enjoined, curriculum. "I declare you an esteemed Archon of the Arts," Pettibone grandly pronounced. "Come to Parami and impart your wisdom."

Axis was put in charge of Performance Focus, although she had not been in front of an audience since the chemically induced night that brought about a permanent terror of setting foot onstage.

Philip Pristley was working as a barista at a coffee shop owned by his girlfriend and her family in Vancouver, BC, when one momentous afternoon, Axis stepped up to the counter and ordered a triple-shot vanilla latte. She was in Canada for a post-punk symposium, which Philip planned to attend. He got her attention by reciting the lyrics to "Call It Desire, Call It Dissolution," one of her lesser-known album cuts. That night, over several pints at a post-punk, post-gathering, Philip, keenly aware that Axis was a preceptor at Parami, asked if she'd ever taught a class on her own lyrics.

By the following morning, the two of them entangled in Axis's room in the Sylva Hotel, it was settled. Philip would come to Parami to teach the seminar Axis: The Lyrical Poetics of the High Priestess of Punk. To further seal the deal, upon Philip's arrival in Pearl Handle, they promptly went to the courthouse and got themselves hitched.

The marriage came to a thud after Pristley took a female undergraduate out for coffee, told her she was developing some very intriguing material, and closed in with: "Have you ever considered an Immersive Study?"

Getting free of Pristley proved more difficult than Axis had estimated. Popular with students, particularly female students, he had joined the Chamber of Wisdom, guaranteeing him opportunities to charm the rarified levels of Parami's power structure. Axis had to adjust to Pristley being appointed Archon of Hybrid and Theoretical Studies, removing him from her Performance Focus.

She vowed to never again let a vanilla latte pass her lips.

IN THE AREA outside the Presider's office, the newly hired and freshly designated Protocol Facilitator, Kevin, a towheaded mid-twenties male, greeted Aaron with: "Doctor Moses will be with you as soon as he concludes his current preceptor interview. Would you like a cup of chai? If you haven't tried it yet, it's truly awesome."

"No thank you," said Aaron.

A couple of minutes later, a gangly fellow in his sixties stepped out of the Presider's office, face flushed and jaw slack, the look of someone who'd just completed an exhaustive run.

"Doctor Moses will see you now," announced Kevin, before needlessly ushering Aaron to the half-opened door.

The office had a muted, sanctuary quality. Behind the Presider's desk hung a massive reproduction of the Last Supper, softly illuminated from the base of the frame. Aaron was so surprised to behold it in the context of Parami, he stopped moving.

Noting his response, the Presider said, "Da Vinci. A true artistic genius, wouldn't you agree?" He motioned for Aaron to step over to the corner of the room where two chairs faced each other: the Presider's seat, a comfy-looking armchair; the other, smaller, straight-backed and wooden. Given the seating arrangement and the Presider's height advantage, Aaron had the not-so-comforting sense of being looked down upon. "Sorry we haven't had the pleasure of meeting until now, Mr. Motherway, I'm just trying to get the lay of the land."

Aaron was still attempting to settle into the brittle chair. "Well, as I'm sure you know, I'm new here myself."

"Yes, Doctor Dillard appointed you in what I believe was his last act as Parami's Presider. He must have felt you possessed some special knowledge or acumen vis-à-vis the Arts Program."

"I had no idea Doctor Dillard would be retiring."

"Most unexpected." Moses pulled a miniature tin of Altoids from the breast pocket of his gray silk suit and popped one into his mouth. "I understand you've been batting things back and forth with your facilitator. Are you all suited up and ready for classes to start?"

"Unfortunately, doctor, we already have a bit of an issue."

Aaron pulled the petition from his suede shoulder bag and handed it to Moses, whose eyes scanned the document with what Aaron took to be a trace of amusement before handing it back. "I suggest you ignore this and get on with your work. This kind of infighting doesn't serve the university."

"I agree, Doctor Moses. But I've got a big job ahead, and a colleague is actively undermining me. I haven't even met most of the students."

"Let's not forget that Mr. Pristley has been a preceptor for two decades and you and I are both new kids on the block. I'm certain there are plenty of people who just need to get to know us."

"Respectfully, sir, this petition seems personal, and I take it very personally. In fact, because of him, I suggest a change be made to the *Preceptor Compendium*." Aaron consulted the printout he'd brought with him. "Page one-fifty-three, paragraph two, under the Dual Interaction Policy: 'No preceptor shall conduct an intimate relationship with any student while dispensing instruction to said student which would result in determining and posting a letter grade.'"

Moses looked vaguely surprised, leading Aaron to the thought that Parami's new Presider had yet to peek at the compendium himself.

"Pristley's way around that is, he woos a female student during one of his scheduled courses, then proposes an Immersive Study which, not stated here, are graded pass-fail. That lack of a letter grade serves as his loophole. No matter what the topic, it inevitably turns into Romance 101. He does this infamously, year-in, year-out; you could set the academic calendar by it."

"My understanding is that Philip Pristley is currently involved in a committed relationship with a mature adult."

"Yes, sir, Regina Coyne, a Timmons Trustee."

"Let's hope that with Ms. Coyne, he's found what he's been looking for all along."

"*Mrs.* Coyne. And what are you going to do when he cheats on Parami's biggest donor, and she pulls her funds from the university?"

Moses leaned back in his massive chair. "What are you proposing?"

"I'd like the compendium to be promptly amended, and for you to back me up when Pristley breaks that rule this fall or spring and I tell him to take his act someplace else."

Moses offered a wan smile. "That strikes me as entrapment, but I will put it under consideration."

The Presider shifted his weight, subtly conveying a change of topic.

"We have an entering freshman, Nolan Hale Pickering, whose mother accidentally shot and killed the boy's father, a tragedy of biblical proportions. He's registered for one of your classes, and you've been designated as his preceptor-guide. You will be receiving a special accommodations document from our newly designated Student Success Division. In light of what the boy is enduring, you'll need to generate a weekly assessment of his progress and overall state of mind."

Aaron, experiencing a spreading flame of resentment, said, "Respectfully, doctor, I don't feel qualified to offer those kinds of responses. That sounds like an extreme case, and I'm not a psychiatrist."

"I'm not under the impression that you're anything of the kind. You're simply being asked to keep an eye on the young man and fill out a weekly report." Rearranging himself in his armchair, Moses said, "Another thing you and I should be talking about is that Parami students have a higher than acceptable rate of withdrawal and leaves of absence. I'm going to head up a task force concerned with whether a student who is applying is likely to cut and run once we get them here. Once that's done, I will personally oversee the admissions process, not only for the overall university, but for every degree program and focus as well . . . You're looking at me funny, Mr. Motherway."

"Again, respectfully, doctor, I don't think that's a good idea."

Moses folded his hands and brought them to his lips.

Aaron continued. "The skill set for creative work is different from that of, say, Zen Studies or Embodied Somatics. The Arts Program should monitor its own applications, as well as the decisions as to who we'll allow in."

"Parami is a tuition-reliant institution. We need those dollars to keep coming, not dry up due to a higher than acceptable dropout rate. In the past, while we may have determined who will come here, there's been little or no consideration as to who will *stay* here.

"Psychology may not be your field, Motherway, but temperament and maturity are qualities we need to start considering. Allow me to be frank about the particulars of your one-year interim appointment. I don't know why Doctor Dillard hired you. Frankly, my own presence here signals somewhat of an institutional departure. I've met individually with longtime staff and preceptors. Some have chosen to jump ship. I understand that and can deal with it, bring in some fresh perspectives, including fresh hires. But you're in a kind of no-man's-land. As an interim appointee, you have a year to prove yourself essential to this institution." Moses smiled but there was no warmth in it. "I will be reviewing, evaluating, and deciding upon all applications. Now, something else just transpired that's going to have an effect upon your program."

CHAPTER 14

Happy Yom Kippur

Aaron returned to Timmons House, simmering. Viti was at her desk in the outer office writing in a tiny notebook, which she closed and pushed aside as Aaron approached. "How did it go?" she asked.

"Did you have any inkling that C. Edmund Northrup and Isadora Chappington were about to take early retirement?"

"Retirement? They're our two youngest preceptors." Viti appeared uncharacteristically flustered. "An email came in from them while you were gone." She clicked her mouse. "Let's see. . . . Northrup and Chappington want to meet with you, soon as possible."

"To explain why they're bailing at the twenty-third hour?"

Her expression shifted, a light coming on. "I'll bet it's about the Northrup-Chappington Lecture Series, the thing they're most involved with. Even if they're leaving, I can't see them letting go of that." She opened the top drawer of her desk, then handed Aaron a glossy brochure. "These are promotional materials, printed and paid for. The lecturers have signed contracts and everything."

"Get back to them and set up that meeting for me. Make it for this afternoon if you can." Aaron handed Viti a slip of paper. "Here are the names of the two new preceptors Moses hired to take their place. Please find out what you can about them."

C. EDMUND NORTHRUP and Isadora Chappington functioned as a tag-team, neither of them doing anything without the other. Their alliance dated back to "The Deduction Poem." C. Edmund was, at the time, employed as an IRS agent, based in Omaha. He met Isadora when she was teaching adjunct at a community college, and her tax form came up to be audited. She was making hardly any money, so there wasn't much of a potential penalty. But C. Edmund (Carl as he was known in those days) harbored literary ambitions and had not met anyone who identified themselves on their W-4 as: *The poet, Isadora Chappington.*

Isadora's audit got sorted out by the two of them in postcoital glow on her couch, scraps of receipts littering the coffee table, cowriting "The Deduction Poem":

> *When I buy a Starbucks while reading Ezra Pound,*
> > *that's a deduction.*
> *When I go to Barnes and Noble and just have a look around,*
> > *that's not a deduction.*

Widely anthologized, a lot of writers consulted it, especially around tax time.

The two of them became not only a couple, but steadfast collaborators, teaching in tandem, poetry as well as essay, their sights always trained beyond the borders of Parami and Pearl Handle.

Twice a year—once in the fall, once in the spring—they would invite an established or up-and-coming writer to Parami. It wouldn't matter what form the writer worked in, as long as there was some amount of fame to rub off on the couple.

They would have Viti arrange transport from a Denver car service, to be driven from Denver to Pearl Handle, then from Pearl Handle back to Denver so the hosts could greet whomever they'd invited, at Denver International Airport.

The lectures were always on Friday night, and student attendance was mandatory. A catered dinner at the Northrup-Chappington residence would take place beforehand, with selected students enlisted as servers, discouraged by the hosts from conversing with the visiting writer.

The Saturday after the lecture, C. Edmund and Isadora would entertain the distinguished visitor on their own, usually with a mild trek in the foothills followed by an elegant, intimate restaurant meal, which, like all other expenses, would be charged to the Arts Program. On Sunday, they would brunch, then accompany the guest to the airport for a glowing farewell. The couple's next coauthored chapbook of poetry or batch of essays would inevitably include an exclamatory blurb from some writer they'd hosted.

After Viti informed Aaron that C. Edmund and Isadora had agreed to come to the office at two that afternoon, he looked over the lecture series brochure and asked Viti, "This guy scheduled for the Spring Passage, why would they invite him?"

"Warren Hyde produces events, mostly tributes to high-profile artists. They're undoubtedly bringing him out hoping he'll invite them to New York to take part in one at some point in the future."

"Did you see the topic Hyde's coming here to present?"

"Yes."

"Don't you find the content a little surprising?"

Viti smiled. "Not much surprises me anymore. If you're thinking of pushing back, Aaron, with all the buttoning up they've done for their lecture series, I wouldn't expect them to go quietly."

AARON WAS SEATED in the Absorption Room when the pair arrived at twenty minutes after two. C. Edmund wafted in first. He was, Aaron guessed, in his mid-thirties. What struck him was C. Edmund's height, which only exceeded five feet owing to his cowboy boots. Tucked in them were blue jeans whose creases gave the impression of having been steam pressed just moments before. Aaron's eyes worked his way up to a huge gleaming belt buckle. C. Edmund wore a white dress shirt, atop of which was an intricately patterned silk ascot. His lips were pursed and his skin drawn tight as though he'd had some early work done. Close-cropped hair Aaron figured to have gone prematurely silver, then tinted blonde.

Isadora Chappington came in behind her partner. In pink flats, she was over six feet tall, alarmingly thin, stick-like arms and legs and neck, all of which moved with the irregularity of a Claymation figure. Her rust-shaded shift hung from her frame. Chin-length, silver, tinsel-like hair framed a smile artificially brightened like a light ignited by motion. "Hello, Aaron Motherway. I'm so sorry we won't be teaching for you this year," she trilled, wrapped in some hybrid accent that Aaron couldn't tell was authentic or assumed.

He motioned for the two to sit across from him at the table. "That came about quite suddenly."

"Well," she continued, "it may seem like not much happens around Parami, but when it does, it happens fast."

Aaron glanced at C. Edmund who looked as if he was ready to spit out something dissolving bitterly behind his pursed lips. "Since you're not teaching for us anymore," Aaron asked, "why did you want a meeting?"

Isadora moved in her chair as though she felt something lodged between her butt cheeks. "The Northrup-Chappington Lecture Series. Although we're all boxed up to move to San Francisco, we're here to assure you not to worry, we're committed to continuing it."

Aaron looked at Isadora, then at C. Edmund. "I'm surprised you think that's still going to happen. The first event you booked, we need to cancel immediately. Since you made the arrangements, I hope you'll also make the call telling"—he glanced down at the brochure—"Emma Dabney that she won't be coming to Parami from"—glancing down again—"Bermuda, is it?"

Isadora, clearly astonished, glanced at C. Edmund, who was staring sphinxlike at Aaron. "We can't cancel Emma," she said, her voice pitched higher. "She runs one of the most prestigious art colonies in the world. She'll be furious with us."

"You should have been more aware of your scheduling. In the *Preceptor Compendium*, which I'm sure you're familiar with, it says that students have the option of not attending classes that are held on days that conflict with their religious or cultural beliefs. By making attendance mandatory, your events are inherently curricular. For the one you have planned the first Friday of October, there's no opportunity for those students to make it up."

"But it isn't a class," Isadora said.

"Yom Kippur. You can't hold an event at that time; it's discriminatory to our students who are Jewish."

Isadora sputtered, then spoke. "We've already prepaid Emma's plane ticket." She reached down and groped for her handbag with the distress of one being held up at gunpoint. "We brought along the receipt to be reimbursed."

"I hope you haven't purchased a ticket for the spring event because that's not going to happen either."

Isadora's lips were trembling as her eyes flooded with frustration or anger or grief, or a swarm of all at once. "And what religious holiday falls at that time?"

"Frankly, I find the content described on your brochure to be unsupportable." Aaron stood. "Now if you'll excuse me, I need to set about integrating two new preceptors."

The couple rose as though each were climbing out of a sickbed. Shuffling to the door, C. Edmund, projecting seething impudence, spoke for the first time, his voice tight and acrid. "We've mentioned you to people in New York, and nobody's heard of you there."

Isadora, lagging behind, turned to Aaron. "Well," she said, face scarlet, lower lip trembling. "Have a happy Yom Kippur."

CHAPTER 15

Lady Luck

Madlenka Kovacs was keenly aware that Stamford had been too afraid not to take her to Pearl Handle, fearful she would tell someone he'd toyed with her, then tossed her away. She'd come to America in 2010 after meeting a widower from Iowa on the internet and marrying him. The marriage lasted only seven months, but she became a citizen, albeit one stuck in Greensboro.

But Pearl Handle didn't seem much better. She loved the physical beauty of the mountains, yet the people seemed spoiled and self-important, preoccupied with their own concerns. While many of the residents came from someplace else, Madlenka still felt she would always be treated as an outsider. Was it her accent, the way she dressed? At least the people back in Iowa, while limited, were down-to-earth.

The job Stamford had gotten Madlenka in Parami's Commerce and Prosperity Sector was unlike any she'd had. Ensconced in a cubicle a couple of miles from the main campus, her duties included tracking the rising and falling rates of investments that Parami held. Among these were an organic farm, various residences that Parami would rent out when they weren't being occupied by visiting preceptors or esteemed guests, a chai company, a factory that made clothing and handbags out of hemp, and a Waldorf middle school. All funds, profits, and expenditures were housed in the Conscious Credit Union, the perennially struggling Parami-founded institution that had long overseen the university's fluctuating fiscal resources.

Madlenka's supervisor, Parami's Archon of Commerce and Prosperity, was a severe and largely silent Thai woman in her sixties named Ratana. Looking over the previous year's instructional and operational budgets, Madlenka swiftly realized she would be helping to maintain a conveyor belt, moving line items from one department to the next, funds which had been earmarked, but were thus far not being used for designated projects or scheduled events.

Ratana's approach to finance was self-devised and woefully arcane. For instance, Madlenka's job called for her to reimburse staff and preceptors for their petty cash expenditures. Employees were made to take each receipt and tape it to an 8 1/2" x 11" sheet of paper, then fill out a form with a space below each item to record the amount and reason for the transaction, who was involved, and how it could be reconciled within the departmental budget. These forms, Madlenka quickly realized, were never reviewed or questioned, the arduous act of filling them out, taken as proof of their validity. When Madlenka suggested to Ratana that for the impending fiscal year, the entire system be transferred to online spreadsheets, she was tersely informed that such innovations weren't welcome.

The other people she worked with, while polite on the surface, were kept too busy to get to know a new coworker in any more than a perfunctory way. As for salary, Madlenka was making less than in Iowa, and the cost of living in Pearl Handle was so inflated there was not much left over.

Back then, at least Madlenka had her trysts with Stamford to sustain her. He'd made it clear that things in Pearl Handle would be different and begged off every time she invited him over. "I'm a university president now and I've been put in place for a purpose. The Lord is depending on me to successfully steer this ship into the harbor."

What do I do with all this free time? Madlenka asked herself.

The first thing was to buy a snazzy four-year-old Subaru and start taking weekend road trips. She quickly discovered that going from one distant Western point to another was an entirely different experience than the America she'd known up to then. She also took up smoking; a few puffs after a meal erupted into a pack and a half of American Spirits a day. One night on the internet, languidly puffing away, Madlenka clicked upon the Redwing Casino, just above the southern Wyoming border, a manageable drive from Pearl Handle.

From the website, Madlenka learned that the casino was located on the Arapaho reservation. The tribe, once over ten thousand strong, had been relegated there by the U.S. government in the latter part of the nineteenth century. After decades of confinement and poverty, just before the turn of the twenty-first century, enterprising tribal members founded the casino, now the largest employer in that region of Wyoming. From casino profits they invested in raising cattle and bison, which also proved to be immensely profitable.

As though heralding her arrival, the place was lit from floor to ceiling with feverish activity. Having never experienced anything like it, Madlenka was enthralled. The drinks were cheap, and the rooms were quite reasonable. Even if you were alone, you could amuse yourself at the slot machines or roulette or blackjack tables. More than once, a man approached her, offering a drink that suggested something further, but Madlenka refused to dilute her attention.

Timid at first, vowing to hold fast to her self-allotted hundred dollars, Madlenka found that luck embraced her, slot machines spitting back winnings, roulette wheels clicking in her favor, cards turning over with the welcoming ease of a lover turning back the sheets.

Although her bets were modest at first, no more than a dollar for the slots, three dollars for roulette and five for blackjack, Madlenka was seen as lucky; poker players slipped her chips or cash just to have her hang at the table. After trying a few hands of poker, her initial choices were what she stuck to, wagers that went fast and whose outcomes were immediate. By Saturday night, her bets ranged from five all the way to fifty, and late Sunday afternoon, Madlenka was astounded to find herself twelve thousand seven hundred and seventy-nine dollars ahead.

At work on Monday, feeling empowered, she all but insisted that Stamford come to lunch at her rented duplex.

ON HIS WAY to Madlenka's, Stamford felt pensive and tense. Visiting Madlenka at her residence risked starting the affair up again. Her summons had an undercurrent, the way she'd insisted he bring her along to Parami, and he found that unsettling. Of the options Stamford felt he had regarding his former mistress—and former is how he considered her—getting her a job at Parami and keeping her at arm's length seemed the least combustible.

Besides this irksome aspect, Stamford felt the takeover of Parami was lining up smoothly. The trick was to target which challenges needed to be addressed immediately, and which of the ridiculous elements and practices that had embedded themselves were, for the time being, best left alone.

Roger Bayne Whitney was discreetly getting the word out to faith-based institutions that an influx of staff, faculty, and students was needed at Parami. So far, Moses felt secure that Parami's heathens, so myopic, self-absorbed, and overburdened, weren't conscious of the wave that would soon be washing over them. The old guard who'd been paid off to depart—and that included Terence Dillard as well as a handpicked set of key staff and preceptors—had adhered to the nondisclosure agreements they'd signed upon receiving their handsome severance. Expensive, yes, the entire venture, but not as much as it would be to break ground and construct an entirely new campus.

One piece that troubled Stamford was why Terence Dillard had brought in Aaron Motherway; why the departing president would go out of his way to install someone new to run the Arts Program, someone who previously had no connection with Parami, or even academia.

Stamford didn't much care for Motherway in the exchanges they'd had. Good thing he'd be gone after the expiration of his one-year contract. That program was one that had some heft out in the world and Stamford was set on transforming it. To that end, he'd brought in two instructors from solid Christian backgrounds, each of whom had temporarily lost their footing. Stamford felt confident that in very little time and with the crop of like-minded students he was recruiting, these two key players would right themselves and set about establishing a faith-based program, sure to make a fresh and wholesome and lasting mark out in the secular world.

Stamford pushed Madlenka's bell at twelve thirty, exactly on time. She greeted him in a provocative sweater and skirt, but then every outfit of Madlenka's struck him as provocative. After dispensing a kiss on the cheek, he acclimated himself to the scene, all the while keeping his distance as though she carried something contagious. "Quite a spread you've prepared," he said as he sat down at her table.

"Whole Foods. Unsure what to serve so I bought different little things. I am so pleased you found time, Mr. Presider. I hardly glimpse you anymore."

"Parami certainly fills up one's dance card, as I'm sure you've discovered. How are things going in your neck of the woods?"

"I am basically a—what you call that kind of bee that possesses no real power?"

"A drone?"

"Drone, yes. Am overqualified for what I am expected to do. And since I am never given real responsibility, everyone assumes I can do nothing."

Stamford grimaced slightly, but beyond that, didn't respond.

"How is your takeover coming, your little bloodless coup?"

"Maddy, you can't mention that to anybody." He looked sternly at her. "You haven't, have you? Mentioned anything?"

"Who would I tell?

"I only told you about it back in Iowa when I never dreamed you'd be coming along." Stamford offered a wan smile. "You can see how different this is from that time. How different things are."

"What happens once you have overtaken Parami? How different will that be?"

"I'll surely be moving on to other challenges, more of the Lord's work." He smiled again. "Look at this sumptuous table you've set, and we haven't even had a bite. Let's say grace."

Madlenka rose and left the room. When she returned, she had a cigarette in one hand and a blue plastic lighter in the other.

"Whoa, what's this?" asked Stamford, as Madlenka fired up the lighter and pressed the flame to the tip. He stood as though he'd spilled something all over himself. "I'm a Christian minister. I can't go back to those heathens smelling of smoke, any more than I could go back there reeking of perfume. Everyone at school will think I'm spending my lunch hour in a bar or at a whorehouse."

Madlenka glared at him, a feeling rising up that had been shoved down and kept there ever since Stamford stepped back from her. The lighter sailed across the room and struck him full on the forehead. He cried out, his hand going up to his face. When he pulled it away, he was relieved there was no sign of blood. He and Madlenka stared at each other. Leaning down slowly, he picked the lighter off the carpet, then looked at the chintzy blue plastic, the words *Redwing Casino* in silver glitter. "I think you dropped this," he said, handing it back to her. "Thank you for making lunch. Hope you enjoy it."

Tears filling her eyes, Madlenka watched as Stamford walked out the door, carefully but firmly closing it behind him.

New Hires

One of Parami's new writing preceptors was Randall Hendricks; the other, Frances Thrush. Hendricks had served on the faculty of Beloved Savior College in Vincennes, Georgia, until the previous May. The most comprehensive information about him appeared on the *Vincennes Daily Bugle*'s website under the headline: Beloved Savior Professor Terminated. The gist of the poorly written article was that Hendricks, thirty-seven, had been on "institutional probation" for self-publishing a book of short stories titled *Noises in the Dark,* which dealt with "goblins, sorcery and the dark elements the college considers to be satanically infused."

While on probation, Hendricks continued publishing such material in an online journal, *Goth: Tales of Blood and Mischief,* under the pseudonym P. H. Krafty. When he won a Spooky, celebrating the best web-based horror and gothic material of that year, he was cell-snapped at an awards banquet in Baltimore. It inevitably appeared on the internet and a colleague ratted him out to the administration. Although fired, Hendricks would, clearly through machinations piloted by Stamford Moses, now be teaching at Parami.

A three-year-old faculty page from Upper Idaho University listed Frances Thrush as having taught English composition and English literature, as well as having served as director of the writing center. Aaron urged Viti to get on the academic grapevine and probe further. An hour later, Viti stepped into Aaron's office, clutching some printed pages, looking pleased with herself.

"Thrush resigned three years ago after a controversy at the National Association of Writing Programs. While on a panel, she read an excerpt from her work-in-progress titled Call Me Joan of Auburn: The Autobiography of Harriet Tubman."

"How can you write someone else's autobiography?"

Consulting one of the printouts, Viti said, "Here's her statement: 'Harriet's story is an important one which deserves to be told in a way that is acceptable to the widest possible readership, told by someone literate, formally educated, and an actual writer.' It created a scandal at the conference, especially among African American attendees. UIU asked her to write an apology and she resigned instead, then couldn't get hired anywhere. She's been living at her parents' home in Colorado Springs, where her father's an evangelical minister."

Aaron had no idea what these two new instructors were capable of teaching. Moses, via email, instructed Aaron to let them separately assume the load that Northrup and Chappington had been co-teaching and allow them to create generic literature and writing courses of their own. *"Although this represents offerings that are not in the current catalog,"* Presider Moses wrote, *"I have decided to allow an exception to policy so that these new preceptors can establish the classes that will inaugurate their own unique perspectives and contributions to the program."*

RANDALL HENDRICKS TURNED up at Aaron's office in a T-shirt and cut-offs, sockless, with a pair of Reeboks that appeared ready for the bin. His unruly beard was flaked with food crumbs—Doritos, Aaron surmised, as the man was clutching an open bag of them. Curly, chalk-dusted hair wafted out beneath an Atlanta Braves cap. Knowing Hendricks's first session was an hour from that moment, Aaron resisted asking if the man really intended to conduct a class dressed like that. It was a slow start as Hendricks, sprawled out in a chair, seemed decidedly nonverbal.

"Your course descriptions are pretty general," said Aaron. "So, I hope you've included details in your syllabi."

"I guess I can do that."

"You haven't completed them yet? You're supposed to provide a copy here, and to Academic Engagement, before you teach your first class."

Hendricks rearranged his bulk, crossing his legs, which were fishbelly white. "Reverend Moses told me not to worry about it. This was all so last-minute, I'll need more time if I'm really going to do that. It's not real complicated. The lit courses, I'll just have them read and we'll discuss topics and I'll assign papers on the texts. The writing course should be just straightforward workshopping."

This response was delivered devoid of inflection or enthusiasm and took forever to complete. "May I ask you something?"

Hendricks shrugged.

"How did Doctor Moses go about hiring you, did you respond to a posting? What was the process?"

"He knew one of the professors at my former school."

"Beloved Savior?"

"Yeah, uh huh."

"Are you acquainted with the other instructor Doctor Moses is bringing in, Frances Thrush?"

"Kind of. I met her at some . . . I mean, I've met her."

"Her first class is this afternoon. I've been emailing her, and she hasn't replied."

Hendricks smiled. "I think she isn't that wild about coming here."

"If she doesn't want to come, why the hell did she accept the position?"

The smile turned grim. "You'll have to ask her." With what looked to be a good deal of effort, Hendricks pushed out of his chair. "I'll pull my syllabi together, then email them to you."

He shuffled to the door, and Aaron was freshly reminded that the man resembled an eight-year-old on his first day of camp.

CHAPTER 17

Indications

Nolan Pickering had been in Pearl Handle over three weeks, relieved to have fled Virginia and his mother's pending court case. A week after he arrived, it came out that Joel Pickering had been having an affair with a twenty-nine-year-old lobbyist named Prudence Waithe. Nolan knew too well that Prudence had served briefly as his nanny a decade before. Although Nolan didn't tell anyone, he'd heard his parents shouting at each other around the time of Prudence's dismissal. The revelation shone poorly on Joel, but also indicated that Bev had a tangible motive, and the state charged her with second-degree murder. Lead attorney Gil Stottlemeyer suggested a plea of manslaughter, but Bev wouldn't have any of it and fired him, hiring other counsel. No, she was sticking to her story, mistaken identity, thought it was a prowler, was guilty of nothing more than protecting herself and her son.

Now there was going to be a trial, and that meant Nolan would have to sit up there in front of everyone and say that of course it made sense his mother reacted the way she did; who wouldn't, out in the middle of nowhere with no protection? Nolan feared that on the stand he wouldn't be able to help his mother's story hold up, and she needed Nolan to keep her out of prison. It was all too much.

Nolan heard that pot had just become legal in Colorado and decided to take a bus fifty-five miles to cross the state line and check it out for himself. When he got to Fort Collins, he went straight to the Can-Abyss Cottage. In the tight lobby, a young woman was behind the counter. "I'm Indica, welcome to the cottage. Your first time with us?"

"Um, yes. Why do you ask?"

"You look like you might need a little guidance. Before you go into the Jungle Room to make your selection, I thought I could offer up a few tips." She handed Nolan a pamphlet. "There's basically two categories, Indica and Sativa."

"And your *name* is Indica?"

She beamed. "My parents were growers. Illegal, back in the day, but now it's all out in the open. Do you have much experience with herb?"

"Smoked it a couple times. It didn't do much for me."

Which was true. His closest friend, Michael Whitehall, used to keep pot inside his monopoly set. The first time, it scorched Nolan's throat and he came down with bronchitis. The second time, he got dizzy and had a headache through an entire weekend.

"We have joints and dab pens," she said, her voice all but singing, "gummy bears and lollipops. Topicals, tinctures, and teas. Do you think you'll want to smoke or chew or lick or rub or sip?"

"I don't think I want to smoke it."

Indica giggled. "You strike me as a licker. When you go in the room, tell them you want a lollipop. But only take a couple of swipes the first time. If you eat the whole thing, you might find yourself going to the mind movies, and something tells me you're not ready for that. Can I have your driver's license?"

"Why?"

"You need a picture ID for the Jungle Room. Don't worry, you'll get it back."

"I don't have a driver's license. I'm new here. I live up in Pearl Handle.

Wait, I have something." Nolan reached into his pocket.

When she saw what he'd produced, Indica's face went bright again. "I went to Parami myself. I'm on a leave of absence, but someday I'll make it back there." With what appeared to be profound intensity, she studied the laminated card. "What's it say here? April twenty, nineteen ninety-three. Happy birthday, Nolan Pickering, you made the cut."

Nolan looked back at her, thrown by the fact that his November, ninety-six, birthday didn't appear on his temporary student ID.

"Tell you what," Indica said, "I'm gonna give you a little welcome to the West present. But like I said, don't gulp the whole thing at once. Don't want you to freak out and never come back. If you like it, you can deal with me directly from now on and not have to go in the Jungle Room or anything. I'm here every day but Tuesday." Indica dropped the multicolored sucker in a plastic bag and handed it to Nolan. "I think you'll find out for yourself," she beamed, "that this part of the country has some of the highest peaks in the nation."

BESIDES BUS TRIPS to the Can-Abyss Cottage, Nolan mostly stayed in his apartment, barely unpacking, trolling the internet, and watching waste-of-time movies. Having skipped Acclimation week altogether, it was the first day of classes, and his first course was titled Groundbreaking Narratives: Novels that Defined Their Moment, taught by someone named Aaron Motherway.

Nolan got out of bed, went to the closet. Hanging were three short-sleeved shirts; one light blue, one beige, and one with red-and-white stripes. He had two long-sleeved shirts, one white and one with green-and-white pinstripes. A pair of khakis and a pair of black dress pants. Nolan did not own a necktie or any kind of scarf or hat. He had two pairs of blue jeans, one in the dresser and one wadded up on the floor. A dozen T-shirts, all plain, no graphics or writing, in black, white, and gray. His eleven socks (five pairs, one extra) were white, made of cotton, as were his half-dozen pairs of briefs. He did not own a suit or sport coat or any kind of jacket. He owned a pair of brown leather slip-on shoes he never wore and a pair of faded black Converse All Stars. He did have a beige trench coat that needed to be dry-cleaned. He didn't know where to get any dry-cleaning done in Pearl Handle and didn't feel like trying to find out. Nor did he want to go looking for a laundromat and didn't want to use the laundry room in his apartment complex.

The one and only time he'd been in there, a goth young woman he'd seen in the hallway was watching her clothes rotate in the dryer. He pulled his laundry out of a plastic garbage bag and one of his pairs of underwear, turned inside out, skid marks in glaring view, plopped on the cement floor. "Sweet," he'd heard her say. Nolan snatched up the briefs, shoved them in the bag, and rushed back to his apartment.

He wished he could wear the clothes he owned until they got too worn and dirty, then go to one of those cheap-ass stores where they didn't pay the people who worked there anything, much less the people who made the clothes overseas, and just buy new ones until they needed to be replaced.

His mother had given him some money and opened a Pearl Handle bank account for him. She told him he'd have to make it last until he got a job while going to school. "These lawyers are bleeding us dry," she offered, by way of explanation.

Since he slept as much as sixteen hours a day, there was no job in the world Nolan wanted or could imagine himself doing or even applying for.

Nolan stood facing the closet. His eyes lit upon one item he'd previously overlooked, a scarlet cloth bathrobe his mother bought for him before he left. He'd tried it on the evening she presented it to him and he liked the way the cloth felt against his skin and the loose, easy way it hung on his slight frame.

He reached for the bathrobe and yanked it from its hanger. He had on only the briefs he'd slept in and a pair of white cotton socks. Once the bathrobe was enwrapping his body, Nolan pulled on both ends of the sash and tied it around his waist. Yes, he liked the way it felt.

He stepped over to his pair of Converse and tugged on the right one, then the left, without fastening the laces. He looked down at his dismal blue jeans, tangled on the floor. He was sick of the way they clung to his legs. The bathrobe felt soothing, screw what anybody thought.

Not caring what the weather was like, Nolan grabbed his camouflage backpack and pulled open the door. He walked down the hallway, dim at all hours, and stepped outside, en route to his first Parami class.

CHAPTER 18

Ashes

Once classes were underway, Aaron discovered how busy he was and was going to be. As part of his Fall Passage load, he was granted four credit hours of release to run the Arts Program, which meant he'd be teaching two classes. The tsunami of email was enough to make him dizzy, two to three hundred messages a day. Aaron had never managed such a deluge. Navigating it was like maneuvering among a crowd whose faces and attire were identical. Yet Aaron opened each one and dutifully deleted or kept it, aware that each message, whether urgent or inconsequential, presented itself on his screen in precisely the same font. Spam that had slipped through—Rolex replicas or massage therapy or male enhancement—looked the same as the announcement of a crucial meeting Aaron was expected to attend. At Parami, such requests were invariably last-minute. If he went an hour without checking his in-box, the possibility of missing something was palpable. He doubted that fellow preceptors and staff at Parami gave institutional emails, like this one from Stamford Moses, more than a cursory skim.

> Starting this semester, the preceptor governance body, formerly known as the Chamber of Wisdom, will alter its designation so

as not to suggest that there is only one perspective or mode of knowledge. In the spirit of Diversity and Inclusivity, the body will be known as the Chamber of Wisdoms (plural). While Parami in the past has been acutely concerned with Eastern traditions, a fresh interface with the Western creeds that most of us were born into might lead to a greater . . .

One email Aaron kept an eye out for was a reply from the newly hired Frances Thrush. He'd gotten her contact information from Sentient Resources after talking to three different staff persons, ultimately convincing them that—as Ms. Thrush's immediate supervisor—such access might be in order. Yet each message to her private email went unanswered. She was scheduled to teach three different classes that first week, and Viti informed Aaron that Thrush had submitted her rather generic syllabi for Moses's approval, then sent it via registered mail, addressed to Parami Arts Program, and that those classes had indeed commenced. She had not replied electronically, nor returned calls, nor stopped by Timmons House, ignoring all requests for an initial meeting.

On Friday, Aaron placed a call to Parami's Technology Fulcrum. After being passed around, he was finally handed over to Juan, a work-study who, it appeared, might be able to answer his questions.

"One of our recently hired preceptors, Frances Thrush, has she been set up with a computer?"

"She has. I installed it myself."

"And she's been using her Parami email account?"

"I imagine so. I can tap into the global system and see if it's active."

Aaron held on for a moment.

"Yeah, she's been sending and receiving since Monday afternoon."

"That's odd," said Aaron, thinking out loud. "She hasn't responded to any of my messages."

"Hold on, let me run a quick search . . . Okay, that's interesting."

"What?"

"Aaron-dot-M at Parami-dot-edu. She has you blocked."

Aaron thought a moment, some unnamed feeling swirling in him. "Has she blocked anyone else?"

"Let me check . . . nope, looks like you're the only one."

"Can you unblock it?"

"That I can't do."

"I'm the Seat of the program she's part of."

"You'll need to get permission from higher up, probably from Doctor Moses himself."

"You said you installed Frances Thrush's computer. Where is her office?"

"In one of the admin buildings downtown, about as far from the main campus as you can get."

THE DOOR TO Moses's office was wide open, and Aaron looked on as a pair from Parami's ground crew hoisted a large open crate stuffed with what appeared to be Tibetan artifacts—statues, photographs, and framed renderings—through the reception area. Moses himself was holding the door open for them, a palpable beam lighting up his face.

"Just schlup that down to the loading dock, fellows. Mitchell is waiting with a truck, and he'll take it from there."

Once the workers huffed out, Moses turned to Aaron. "Glad you called, Motherway. You apparently have something urgent, and I do as well. Come in, have a seat." Moses sat facing Aaron with hands folded in front of him. "You first."

Aaron recounted Francis Thrush's deliberate effort to keep from communicating with him. All the while, Moses's breezy demeanor was receding.

"So, what are you needing from me, Motherway?"

"Support, sir. How am I supposed to communicate with her if she won't take my calls and has blocked me from her email?"

Moses's brow was furrowed. "Are you sure you *need* to communicate with her?"

"C'mon, doctor. She's being insubordinate."

Moses took a long moment.

"Frances Thrush is an unusual case. She underwent a great deal of trauma after a misunderstanding at her last institution. Was bullied online. Never wanted anything to do with academia ever again. Was, in fact, contemplating the seminary. But she has a lot to offer higher education. If you let her find her way, I'm sure her contribution will speak for itself."

"My understanding is that she made some questionable remarks regarding race."

Moses's frown deepened. "And you feel that I, as an individual of color, should be especially sensitive to that? I believe we should celebrate progress and not dwell on missteps. If you haven't noticed, there's an African American halfway through his second term in the White House. So, thank you for looking out for me, but I believe in second chances, Motherway. Redemption." Moses appeared increasingly solemn. "You should also be aware that the trauma Ms. Thrush suffered is so severe that, due to institutional liabilities, we can't subject her to any dialogue or confrontation that could trigger the deficiency that she is trying to overcome."

"What kind of deficiency?"

"Due to FERPA regulations, I'm not at liberty to discuss that."

Nothing for a moment, then Moses continued with a shift in tone: "As you saw when you arrived here, I'm doing a bit of housecleaning. Old artifacts in storage, antiquated items gathering dust. You wouldn't believe all the stuff, much of it junk, I've been unearthing around here. Oriental kitsch that you might encounter at some sidewalk bazaar." Moses pointed. "And then there's this."

An urn was on the desk, silver with an elaborate graphic, gleaming red stones bordering its base. "I'll bet you'd never guess in a hundred years what's contained in there."

Aaron didn't stir.

"When Willard Pettibone expired, he had no family; had made artistic accommodations regarding his work, but none for his actual remains, beyond his request for cremation. Can you believe the ashes of the late, and so I'm told, *great* artist have been stashed in that safe over there? Some kind of ritual might be in order. Perhaps spreading them in the mountains or in the Pearl Handle River, as I understand the man, albeit from New York City, had an affinity for nature."

No response from Aaron.

"That other stuff, I'm having taken to a recycling facility in Cheyenne. But I thought, well, Pettibone founded the Arts Program, so perhaps you could arrange a ceremony, see that he's dispersed in the midst of some of this region's natural beauty . . . Motherway, you're looking at me strangely."

"Respectfully, sir, my position seems quite expansive, but I don't think spreading human ashes appears anywhere in the job description."

"So, you're refusing your Presider's request?" Clearly annoyed, Moses reached over and lifted a sheet of paper from his desk. "I'm going to be sending this out in email but I'm giving you a hard copy."

Aaron took the sheet without looking at it.

"It's a talk Parami's esteemed founder, Lawrence Timmons, once gave on the subject of gossip. How we, as an institution, should regard that undermining and corrosive element." Moses looked across the desk with what Aaron took to be fervent intent. "Anyone concocting falsehoods, or even their own limited perspectives on university policy, will be subject to censure or dismissal."

Aaron rose without another word, taking the paper with him. Once down the hall, down the stairs and on the outside steps, he saw there was a box stuffed with objects, waiting to be lifted and loaded by Parami's ground crew. He folded the paper, tore it to pieces, then dropped it in the box, atop other materials to be discarded.

CHAPTER 19

Mentorship

Having applied too close to the beginning of Fall Passage, Ophelia Jenks was on what was designated at Parami to be Introductory Track, which meant she would take a limited number of arts workshops before declaring a focus in the spring.

Her poetry class was Sounds Like: An Aural Interpretation of World Poetry taught by Elia Adank. This consisted of reading aloud poems in one of the six-besides-English languages that Adank spoke, then coming up with your own soundalike version of what you felt was the meaning.

She was also enrolled in Feminist Theory and Its Application, taught by Philip Pristley. This had an assigned reading component, and Ophelia, having only attended three sessions, was several chapters behind. While she'd intended to drop the class to avoid failing, Ophelia suspected that the date had already passed.

The only offering that vaguely engaged her was Wit and Wisdom: Reflections of Lawrence Timmons, an immersion into the philosophy of Parami's founder, team-taught by various preceptors. The centerpiece of the course was Timmons's third published work, *The When/Then Book.*

Within the eight hundred eighty-eight printed pages were four hundred forty-four sayings, each starting with When, and concluding with Then. Wanting each pronouncement to be savored, free from competing information, Timmons insisted that the When instruction be placed in the center of its own left page, the Then response identically typeset on the right. Examples:

When you're in a room... Then be in the room
When you're at a party... Then be at the party
When you're drawing a picture... Then draw the picture
When you're reading a page... Then read the page
When you're riding a bike... Then ride the bike
When you're eating an orange... Then eat the orange
When you're smoking a cigarette... Then smoke the cigarette
When you're drinking gin... Then drink the gin
When you're fishing in a stream... Then fish in the stream
When you're lost in the mountains... Then be lost in the mountains
When you have a fever... Then have a fever
When you're taking a crap... Then take a crap

One earnest freshman brought up that such a presentation was ecologically careless. The concern was brushed aside by lead teacher Betsy Cohn: "In some cases, wisdom trumps waste."

Ophelia, longing for the sanctuary of Winnetka, was considering leaving Parami, until one afternoon in the Timmons Library, she happened upon a copy of Axis's coffee table publication *Fisting in Sandusky*, a decidedly firsthand account of the furor around an installation Axis had co-curated with Willard Pettibone.

With the funds from a Koltisch grant, she and Pettibone set about staging and documenting events in Middle America, seeing how far they could push the bounds of prurient interest. The part of the exhibit that received the most attention was a reproduction of three public toilet stalls, replete with glory holes on either side of the one in the center, with an explicit invitation to male museumgoers to work their members into an excited state to be posited accordingly. Once she had taken in ample texts and images and closed the book with a sigh, Ophelia knew what she had come to Parami for: to make Axis her mentor.

OPHELIA WENT DURING posted office hours and found Axis at her desk, a selection of paint swatches in front of her. "I'm transforming this space," Axis said, by way of a greeting. "Which of these colors do you like the most?"

Ophelia looked down. There was lavender but also a mint green that, while one might ultimately tire of it, was striking upon first glimpse. "The green one. Green suggests success and prosperity."

"Of course," said Axis. "So, you're not in any of my classes, are you? Not even a Performance student, correct?"

Ophelia rather timidly shook her head no.

"And you came to see me *because?*"

Ophelia, still hanging by the doorway, stepped deeper into the office. "I'd like to work with you, be . . . I don't know, your assistant."

"I'd need to accept you into our focus, and you'd need to start taking some of our . . . what do you call them, pre-reqs."

"Not a problem. I'll look into declaring before Spring Passage."

"Whoa, if you want to be a Performance student, you'll be needing to make a statement that you're serious."

"Statement?"

"The Student Arts Performance is coming up and I'm in charge. Why don't you prepare a performance piece, then we can talk."

"Isn't that really soon? I can't put anything together that fast."

"Be conceptual. Pull something out of the air." Axis glanced down at the palette spread out on her desk. "You're right, luv. Definitely the green."

CHAPTER 20

Budgets and Bagels

Aaron was in his office, scrolling through his email.

> As you may have noticed, all Parami restrooms are newly designated as non-gender. For the 2014-2015 academic year, in response to more than one concern, the mounted porcelain urinals, originally installed in what were once defined as men's rooms, are considered by many to be male-specific and therefore not in keeping with the spirit of a non-gender facility. Please fill out the accompanying survey (it will take approximately twenty minutes) to indicate your preference as to whether these potentially oppressive stations should be removed or remain in place.

His desk phone rang and Aaron picked it up. "Arts Program."

"Is this Professor Motherway?" A woman's voice with what seemed like an Eastern European accent. "This is Madlenka of Commerce and Prosperity. You have a minute?"

"Sure, what can I do for you?"

"I am tracking unreturned funds from various programs. Have you information concerning petty cash from previous academic calendars?"

"Are you aware that I just got here?"

"Most departments and programs have unused line items from previous budgets. It would be most helpful if you could locate such funds to return here to Commerce and Prosperity."

"It's petty cash we're talking about? I mean, how much could it be? It's my understanding most departments make sure they spend their budgets by the end of each fiscal year, and I'm sure the Arts Program is no exception."

A moment. "You were not here and so you would have no information?"

"That's right."

"Sorry to be a bother."

She hung up and Aaron, looking at the phone, couldn't help shaking his head. He opened his desk drawer and pulled out the Northrup-Chappington Lecture Series brochure. His eyes scanned the text for the spring event. Aaron punched in the number. Half a ring, then a male voice answered, "Warren Hyde here." A rhythmic pulse was populating the background.

"I'm Aaron Motherway, calling from Parami University."

"Okay."

"This weekend practicum you've developed, The Genius of Ted Bundy: How a Serial Killer Concocts a Narrative, is—"

"What about it?"

"—going to be canceled."

"Wait, while I turn this down." The background dipped considerably. "You're looking to reschedule?"

"It's not going to happen."

A moment. "I have a contract."

"Sorry."

"Are you aware that I'm the Director of Bundy Studies at the College of—"

"Students are paying real money to come here, Warren. We will not be offering your class." Another call was coming through as Aaron let Hyde take his final shot.

"Look, shithead, I don't know who you think you're dealing with, but if you think I'm just gonna roll over, you're out of your freaking mind. What was your name again?"

"Motherway, Aaron. I have another call." He pressed the flashing button. "Arts Program."

"Joshua Feldman here." Vice-Presider of Academic Engagement. "How's things on your side of the street?" he asked, exuding palpable warmth.

Aaron, vaguely disarmed, did his best to rally. "We're taking care of business."

"That's what I hear, that's what I hear." The man's voice was practically tuneful.

"Listen, I'd like to stop by with a couple of preceptors you probably haven't met. Do you know Jordy Hurwitz from Zen Studies?"

Aaron didn't.

"Betsy Cohn, from Diversity?"

Again, Aaron didn't.

"Good folks, you should meet. I'll pop by with them at the end of the day. You'll be in your office, I assume?"

Aaron felt thrown off by the call. The preceptor and staff at Parami were, almost to a person, anything but friendly. Most seemed preoccupied, fatigued, or vaguely disgruntled, and here was the second-most influential player on campus, coming on like they'd grown up together.

A few minutes after five, Viti awkwardly ushered Feldman, accompanied by a man and woman, through the front area of Timmons House.

"I've never been in here," said Feldman, with a jovial tone. "I understand we academics aren't especially welcome in the artists' neighborhood."

Aaron joined them in the Absorption Room for introductions.

"This shouldn't take long," crooned Feldman. His sunny mood from earlier seemed not to have diminished.

Aaron looked at the trio of beaming faces. Betsy was around sixty, brown-black hair with a hint of maroon that appeared freshly tinted. Something about her was familiar, and Aaron felt he must have passed her several times on campus. Jordy, around the same age, wore a fedora tipped jauntily to the side. They took the chairs, two of them extra that Viti had provided, then Feldman got right to it.

"Jordy and Betsy and I were talking about you yesterday, as what you did clearly got our attention."

"What did I do?" asked Aaron.

Betsy leaned forward. "For years, none of us have acknowledged how, well, *insensitive* even a Mindful institution such as Parami has been concerning the Jewish holidays."

Jordy weighed in. "I can tell you from experience that only a handful at Parami even know what Purim is. I poll my class around that time and they're almost unanimously clueless."

"And with our new Presider's Christian background, we want to make sure other traditions aren't overlooked," added Betsy.

Where do I know her from?

Jordy again: "Canceling that reading scheduled for Yom Kippur was the kind of step I'm ashamed to say some of us should have taken long ago."

"The administration?" asked Aaron.

Feldman, who had been leaning back in his chair, now smiled with an ever-deepening warmth. "Bu-Jews."

"Beg your pardon?"

"Bu-Jews," said Feldman. "Raised Jewish but practicing Buddhists. There's quite a number of us throughout the university."

Jordy smiled. "We're going to start getting together on Fridays to wish each other Shabbat Shalom, maybe grouse about Parami's goyim."

"There's plenty to grouse about, believe me," said Betsy.

Aaron's memory ignited, and he tried not to visibly react as he remembered where he'd seen her.

Feldman said: "So, you're up for joining in? We thought we might start with a long lunch at Maury's."

Jordy added, "The only place in Pearl Handle that has anything that comes close to back East."

They were all looking at Aaron, who was trying to regain his footing.

"I'd have trouble identifying myself as a—what did you call it—Jew-bu, since I'm not Buddhist and I'm not Jewish. So, I'd feel a little funny calling myself a . . . you know."

Feldman appeared startled. "Not Jewish? But you canceled for the Day of Atonement."

"I just . . . needed a good reason."

Jordy studied Aaron. "You sure you're not Jewish, not on your maternal side, or anything?"

"One always takes the religion of the mother," Feldman added, somewhat incongruously. "You're always sure who your mother is, but you can't be sure about your father."

"I'm sure about my father," Aaron uttered. "And my mother was a lapsed Catholic."

A shift in the room. Then Feldman said, "Sounds like you won't be joining us."

As the two men shuffled toward the door, Betsy Cohn shot Aaron a look, then said, "So, not Jewish, but you appropriated the most solemn day in Judaism for your own purposes?" Over her shoulder, she added, "A *mamzer* among us."

Aaron watched her go. Although, her hair was now without its silver racing stripe, and although Aaron was sure she hadn't recognized him, Betsy Cohn was the woman who had attacked him for tossing an apple core to the ground.

CHAPTER 21

Crustaceans On Canvas

Parami's Plateau Performance Space was another example of a modest element designated much more grandly than it was. As the Parami campus had previously been a hospital, PPS had served as that former institution's cafeteria, a gaping, cavernous room with a high ceiling. Upon one entire side, a stage had been constructed and a set of curtains rigged, but there was no backstage to speak of. The lighting plan, of the coffee can variety, had been installed three decades before. Every significant event was held in the space, and it was booked nearly every night.

For the Student Arts Performance, Aaron sat in back as he'd done during the summer. There was an established practice of reserving the front row for preceptors, guests, and high-ranking administrators. Aaron heard that the students, while cooperating with the policy, grumbled among themselves concerning the hierarchical nature of it. He knew that some students took note of him in the back and saw it as a gesture of solidarity. Aaron preferred the back. If he were to nod off, as had happened more than once, he was less likely to be found out.

The lights, dim to begin with, dimmed even further, and Katryn Burley, the evening's host, ambled onto the stage. Aaron had met Katryn but couldn't say they'd shared a conversation. Seemingly affable and engaging, Katryn went to Academic Engagement almost weekly with some seething complaint, often about Aaron. Katryn served on the Arts Program as a visual artist, in particular a calligrapher, but at some point in recent years decided that country music was the great American form of expression. While she didn't attempt to teach it or anything related to it, Katryn was convinced it was the medium capable of reaching the most people and having the biggest impact on individual as well as global consciousness. Trouble was, her songs were esoteric and totally unsuited to a mass audience, with titles like "Lotsa Bodhisattvas" and "The Bardo or the Boudoir?"

Although from Philadelphia, Katryn had, ever since her foray into her version of Americana, assumed a dustbowl accent. Tonight, Katryn was decked out in a beige Stetson, red kerchief, and bib overalls as she cradled an autoharp. When Katryn commenced strumming, it sounded as though half the strings were sharp and the other half flat, like a set of wind chimes whose effect was unnervingly dissonant.

"Before we bring out our student performers, I thought I'd serenade all y'all with a song I'm proud to say I've had more'n one request for."

"Buddha!" yelled a young male in the audience as Katryn beamed.

"You got it. And what was Buddha besides an enlightened being?"

"A cowboy!" several voices called out in unison.

Backed by her discordant strumming, Katryn crooned in an alto whose tonality suggested more than a passing familiarity with the late Johnny Cash.

Buddha was a cowboy, he rode the Dharma range.
Buddha was a cowboy, to you it must sound strange.
He knew that things were changeless,
But learned to love the change.
Buddha was a cowboy.

Katryn concluded to copious applause, then announced the first act, a set of five upper-level undergrads known onstage and off as the Derridas, the name emanating from twentieth-century French philosopher Jacques Derrida, all the academic rage during the time Aaron was himself an undergrad, and who, somewhat incongruously, served on the faculty at UC Irvine in sunny Orange County.

Being acolytes of Philip Pristley, none of the Derridas had enrolled in any of Aaron's classes. Functioning as a collective, they only took classes as a unit. The Derridas onstage resembled the Derridas in everyday life, having embraced a retro cool-nerd look: the two young men in vests, bow ties, and Clark Kent glasses; the three young women in billowing skirts, anklets, and patent leather shoes. Each wielded an instrument: banjo, clarinet, trombone, claves, and shruti box, the latter being a set of Indian bellows, currently more in evidence at Parami than in India itself.

The Derridas played tunelessly and without any discernible pulse, not once acknowledging the audience. Aaron felt as though he were cocooned in a garage, being overcome by fumes. His memory ignited with a quote from Derrida himself that had stuck with him from a long-ago lit-theory seminar: "To pretend, I actually do the thing; I have therefore only pretended to pretend."

After a ragged and dismal conclusion, the audience rewarded the Derridas with a vigorous ovation.

Then four students came out, three male, one female, and meticulously arranged four oversized colored blocks on the stage—red, green, yellow, blue—and for twenty minutes each delivered one of four mantra-like lines:

> *I am cold.*
> *I am lonely.*
> *I am searching.*
> *I am Sara.*

As the final "I am Sara" lingered in the air, the applause ignited, several of the audience offering whoops and cries.

Cradling her autoharp, Katryn Burley reprised one of her well-loved verses:

> Buddha was a cowboy, he rode the rugged earth.
> Buddha was a cowboy, attuned to rebirth.
> He knew the world was worthless, infused with
>   inner–worth.
> Buddha was a cowboy.

With that, she announced intermission.

When Aaron stepped outside, a couple of students across the way were lighting up cigarettes. One was Trevor, enrolled in Aaron's lit seminar.

"Could I bum one of those?" asked Aaron.

The young man looked surprised. "Sure, Mr. Motherway."

Aaron, unlike all other preceptors at Parami, insisted that the students not call him by his first name—a stab at some kind of protocol.

After lighting up and getting the rush of that first draw, Aaron didn't stay and smoke with the students, but walked away thinking about the presentations he'd just witnessed as well as the audience's response. It was, he felt, like a T-ball game after which every kid was given the assurance that a World Series ring was gleaming in their futures.

When Aaron returned to his seat, there were six young women in frozen poses onstage. Without Katryn assuming the introduction, a recorded track started, then stopped, and Aaron registered that a look of confusion clouded a couple of the performers' faces. A different track kicked in, apparently the right one, because each of the dancers roused from their ice-pose and started moving.

The collective movement didn't seem borne of any choreography, as each of the leotard-clad women appeared to be responding like marionettes manipulated by separate puppeteers. One teetered precariously at the lip of the stage. At first, Aaron felt this was intentional, then figured it wasn't, as the dancer steadied herself with propeller-like movements, before easing backward to safety.

Once the young women assumed what appeared to be their agreed-upon stations, they again struck poses. The musical track became more rhythmic and thunderous as a spotlight probed the rear of the stage. The makeshift curtain parted, and a slight figure came twirling out, clad in a crimson robe, spinning forward. Aaron recognized the robe as the garment perennially worn by Nolan Pickering, the moody, remote kid in his class whose mother had tragically killed his father.

Nolan's movement was awkward but spirited, arms thrust out at ninety-degree angles. He pulled them toward his frame, both hands grabbing the opening at his chest. The robe fell behind him. Underneath, he wore nothing, and his dance became even more feverish, dervish-like. After a series of twirls, he bent forward at the waist, fingers snapping, penis waving, a tiny bobber being tugged atop a mound of moss.

The female dancers broke their poses and swarmed toward Nolan from all directions, enveloping him like the closing petals of a flower. The lights dimmed as Nolan appeared to be shrinking inside the other performers.

When the lights were fully down, the crowd erupted. Aaron clapped dutifully but there was something disturbing about Nolan's fervid but wholly amateurish performance. He recalled a party he'd once attended in high school, the first time he'd seen one of his classmates totally drunk, shouting incomprehensibly, flailing at the air, barely able to stand. What Aaron had just witnessed he took to be a similar cry for help. *What was the kid even doing in school at this time in his young, tormented life?*

With Katryn nowhere in sight and likely, Aaron surmised, no longer in the neighborhood, a pair of student stagehands rolled a sizeable easel to center stage. Another rolled out a media cart and projector. Yet another carried out a small table upon which were a set of objects Aaron could not make out.

Patsy Tilden, a sophomore in the Arts Program, bounced out dressed more stylishly than Aaron had ever seen her. She positioned herself behind a microphone which was immediately adjusted to her small height by one of the efficient, taciturn stagehands.

"Is this on?" Patsy's voice boomed. Glancing at a printout, she commenced her introduction. "Ophelia Jenks, who now goes by simply Opal, comes to us from Chicago, where her commitment to art commenced at an early age and qualified her as a genuine prodigy. Opal's fascination with all things written and visual began with comic books and graphic novels. Her first medium was acrylic but soon she began to incorporate found objects collected from the shores of Lake Michigan to the curio stands and folk art of Maxwell Street."

Aaron tuned out, knowing that Patsy was just getting started. Having been to enough Parami readings and performances over the summer, he was aware that such introductions were a collaboration between the performer and the person chosen to introduce them, the result often being a longer presentation than the performances themselves, like attending a show of balloon tricks where, in advance, the audience had to watch the balloons being inflated.

A modest tremor of applause sent Aaron's attention back to the stage. Opal emerged from stage left, hair spiked in the manner of Axis and tinted equal parts purple and green. She had on a beige smock, the front of which was covered by a white bib. Opal wore a pair of combat boots whose laces had been removed. She stood with no expression as a scrawny male cellist with shoulder length hair, black jersey, and jeans settled into a chair before vigorously attacking the strings. Opal cocked her ear as though leading a jazz ensemble on the stage of some hip nightclub. She stepped over to the table and donned a pair of work gloves before dipping one hand into what appeared to be a fish tank, then came up with a reddish object. Several audience members near the front reacted with responses that ranged from gasps to laughter.

Opal shoved her arm forward as a live lobster writhed beneath the stage lights. Aaron rose from his seat and made his way to the front. By the time he'd arrived at a much-improved vantage point, Opal had dipped the lobster downward to a palette on the table. She stood stoically as the lobster flailed its claws among the array of paints. The projector kicked in and a screen at the back of the stage depicted the image of the lobster, claws tainted with various hues, held in place by Opal as it roamed the surface of the canvas, producing a glob here, a streak there, an amalgam of shapes and colors.

Aaron noted that several others had risen from their seats to get a better look, as the lobster produced its visual statement. Opal continued to impassively dip the lobster claws into the paint. As more of the canvas was being covered or when a particularly inventive stroke was made, some of the audience clapped; others watched in consternation.

Opal lowered the lobster to the canvas, only this time its claws, previously so accommodating, stopped squirming before drooping miserably.

The cellist looked up from his improvised variations. Those who'd been calling out or clapping in encouragement stopped. Opal stood in front of the canvas, composed up to that point, but now clearly at a loss.

Silence, then a voice said: "Is it *dead?*"

The cellist rose from his chair and hauled his bulky instrument from the stage as though he'd spotted flames somewhere in the room.

Opal noted her accompanist's retreat. Aaron, transfixed, regarded her expression as that of a child who'd been baking a cake only to have batter spray all over the walls.

Another voice, this time not with shock but with disgust, said: "Look what she did. She *murdered* the poor thing."

CHAPTER 22

Secondhand Smoke

Madlenka pulled her burgundy Subaru to the front of the Redwing Casino. "Good evening, Ms. Marnie," chimed the young valet.

Madlenka had chosen her casino name after seeing a film with that title on the classic movie channel. "Hello," she said as she stepped out of the car, not smiling as she usually did. No, this weekend was about being focused and resolute, all business.

Her early winnings, like a charmed life devastated by a grave diagnosis, had swiftly plunged below zero, and with every weekend, kept moving with the force of a rockslide or avalanche, devastations common to this region. She'd dropped sixty-five thousand the previous weekend, fifty-five the weekend before, and now was determined to win it all back. To do that, she'd come with as much as she'd been able to pry and scrape from numerous accounts of Parami's Conscious Credit Union, hoping what she considered to be temporary gaps would go undiscovered.

She checked into her room, the one the Redwing had comped for her, brushed her teeth, dabbed on perfume, slipped into the dress she'd just purchased, dashed down to the roulette table, third one on the left, and slapped down three thousand dollars, a pebble dropped into the pond to commence her momentous winning weekend.

HAROLD BLACK KETTLE moved across the faded blue carpet that spanned the casino. How many nights had he walked this floor, taking in the dark red walls beneath the garishly lit ceiling? He could likely calculate close to the exact number, as he'd been a floorperson for twenty-four years. His eyes, once sharp and thorough, were growing dimmer than he cared to admit. His legs, once swift and fluid, now perpetually throbbed and ached as though strapped with some invisible cargo.

A quarter century before, Harold, of the Cheyenne Nation, had been against establishing the casino; he felt it was an affront to the hallowed land of the Arapaho People, with whom the Cheyenne were aligned. But he soon saw the wisdom of doing so.

Whites had flooded to Redwing from the outset, pockets, purses, and fists brimming with cash, their vices begging to be exploited. Once it was the whites who corrupted the Arapaho with whiskey-thirst and all weaknesses of the flesh, but the casino had turned it back on them for profit.

Harold had for years carried a silent joy around with him, probing the faces of the pale visitors, seeing in their eyes that they'd just lost that week's paycheck, that year's bonus, their lifetime savings. But now Harold felt more compassion, a kind of weary tenderness; for, like the whites he once silently disdained, the casino had finally exacted something from him.

Harold had floated through this carnival haze for thousands of nights, absorbing the clouds and fumes of countless cigarettes, which finally caught hold of him. The whites had gotten him after all. Their chemically cured tobacco had poisoned him, and he didn't even smoke.

This would be his last night. He'd tell his boss at the end of the shift that he wouldn't be coming back. None of that two-weeks-notice shit, no going-away party, just a yank of the plug, plunging that very substantial part of his life into darkness. Harold needed whatever time and energy he had left to put things in order.

His attention was seized by a collective groan erupting from one of the roulette tables. That kind of response invariably meant that someone engaged in high stakes had come close but lost. *Oh*, he nearly said out loud, *it's that woman from Pearl Handle.*

She'd been coming since summer and was clearly in a spiral. While Harold was readying for his shift, one of the pit bosses told him she'd gotten here last night and had lost thirty grand on one hand of blackjack.

Harold strode toward the table, picking her out of the throng of spectators. Her face appeared bloodless, wounded. He continued toward the woman, *what was her name, Mary, Marie.* She looked like a child alone on a busy street, facing oncoming traffic. She took a step toward the table, readying herself to place another bet. Harold gently took hold of her elbow. "Excuse me," he said in a low voice. "Why don't you come with me for a moment."

Madlenka followed Harold out of the casino and into the lobby, where there were sofas and tables arranged for players to sit and have coffee or a drink or a smoke.

"Your name is Marie, is that correct?"

Close enough, so Madlenka nodded.

"You are Russian, is that correct?"

Again Madlenka nodded as she, hands trembling, pulled a pack of Spirits from her shoulder bag and lit one up.

"Are you married?"

Madlenka drew in some smoke, pushed it toward Harold. "What business of yours is that?"

"I'm just curious where all the money you're losing is coming from, who else is being affected by you losing it."

"I have plenty of money," she said, cigarette between her lips. "My husband, my *ex*-husband, I should say, is a count. The money from him could not be spent in any lifetime."

Harold nodded, then looked away, partly to better avoid the smoke and partly because she was lying.

"I work here," he told her. "Have for many years. I have never said to anyone what I am about to say to you."

She leaned forward.

"Luck is a light that surrounds certain people at certain times. You don't have it, so you're only going to lose and keep losing. I don't see it coming back to you for a long, long time. Maybe never."

She let out a harsh laugh. "If you work here, why you would tell me such a thing? Is it not your job to make money for the house?"

Harold pushed back his chair. "Like I said, I've never offered a player this kind of advice. I don't know about counts and countesses, but I do know about counting. You're in deep enough already. I hope you don't dig any deeper."

Harold rose from the table and left her there.

Madlenka smoked another cigarette, fighting the fierce urge to go back to the table. *Maybe he is right,* she told herself. *Could be my luck has run out here. There must be other casinos, bigger ones.* She had something left, enough for a modest stake. She just needed the stars to shift, the wheel to turn once again in her favor.

CHAPTER 23

The Poets of Delaware

The death of the lobster, who somebody named Pollock, was captured on video by the Arts Program and on a number of cell phones. Within minutes it was on YouTube and all over social media, and while some comments praised Opal for attempting a bold and singular concept, many denounced her as a monster.

Opal fled the stage in the aftermath of her botched performance, and a student scooped up the lobster, took it home, and tucked it into a shoebox. There Pollock remained as the controversy went viral, and within forty-eight hours, a funeral was held in front of the Timmons Library that included prayers and chanting in hopes that Pollock's journey into the bardo would be peaceful rather than wrathful and chaotic.

The funeral received substantial local attention in the *Pearl Handle Recorder*. As the controversy continued to swell, a group was formed, Sadistic Treatment of Pollock (STOP), calling for Opal's expulsion.

When reporter Harvey Gluck tracked down Opal by phone, the artist herself took a hard line. "I purchased the lobster from the Merchant Seaman, one of Pearl Handle's most popular restaurants. It was going to be boiled and cut up and consumed as a so-called delicacy and you might say that I, by giving the creature the opportunity to participate in an artistic statement, also gave it the opportunity to die with dignity." Then, she couldn't stop herself. "And while we're at it, why don't we ask all those self-righteous meddlers what they had for dinner last night, and if it included slain beef or swine or chicken or trout or cod or catfish or mussels or oysters or shrimp, then they can kiss my meat-eating ass."

When a gallery in Austin asked if she would come and recreate her performance, Opal, now adopting third person self-reference, replied: "Opal is an artist who doesn't repeat herself. Her collaboration with Pollock was a one-off, a Polaroid," giving the impression she was already devising her next performance.

AFTER AARON CANCELLED Warren Hyde's Bundy workshop, the critic posted a protest on *Spoonful* magazine's website. Once a viable alternative cultural resource, *Spoonful* now trafficked almost exclusively in celebrities. Nonetheless, Aaron was attacked by Warren Hyde as: "displaying a blatant disregard for academic freedom as well as freedom of expression."

When he arrived the next morning, Aaron ordered a takeaway breakfast from the Parami food truck, having decided on a response to Hyde's attack. At his desk, the first thing he did was fire up his computer and search "most controversial writer in America." Two of the first three articles that came up were devoted to Rahsaan Jerome Cooke. To Aaron, the name was vaguely familiar, although he'd never read a line of the man's poetry. There was still money in the budget from the defunct Northrup-Chappington reading series, so he rang Viti and asked her to track Cooke down.

"I'm sure I can find him, Aaron, but why do you want to talk to Rahsaan Cooke?"

"I thought I'd invite him to come here and read."

He could imagine Viti gaping at him from the other end of the line. "Why would you do that?"

"Academic freedom," said Aaron. "Freedom of expression."

"Are you aware of his history? He wrote a poem titled "Calling Nine Eleven," which claimed the World Trade Center attacks were just staged to boost the ratings of corporate media. He said it was satire, but few people were amused." Empty air, then Viti said, "I wasn't going to bother you, Aaron, but I've got a call holding I need some help on."

"What's the problem?"

"This guy calls every few months. He's got a fixation on Elia. Will you try and get rid of him?"

She put the call through.

"Arts Program," Aaron said in a monotone.

"Arts Program," said the voice, infused with displeasure. "Does that include your so-called writing program?"

"What can I do for you?"

"To whom am I speaking?"

Aaron took a breath, feeling like one of those Mumbai customer service operators on the wrong end of a complaint. "Aaron Motherway, Seat of the program."

"I already told all this to the girl."

Aaron didn't respond, sensing that whatever this was, he was in for an earful.

"My name is Leslie Kroll and I represent the poets of Delaware. Since I assume you're literate, have your read my glob?"

"Your what?" Aaron jotted the caller's name on a Post-it.

"My glob, sir. I post readings and reviews, of chapbooks mostly, regarding all things poetic in Delaware."

Aaron, trying to get traction, said, "Your *blog*, is that what you're talking about?"

"No, idiot. Everybody and their aunt Dorothy has a blog. Mine is a *glob*. You've never heard of an anagram? I remixed the letters to indicate that what I have is something different entirely."

"That was very clever of you."

"Elia Adank, that slug, that vermin—isn't he one of your so-called preceptors?"

Aaron again didn't respond. No use trying to engage anyone already so wound up.

"This Adank of yours, who calls himself a poet, is scheduled to do a reading in Wilmington on the, let me look here, twenty-eighth of January at some venue I never heard of. But let me tell you, mister, if that whale turd crosses into our region to read what he considers to be poetry, then we have a little surprise brewing for him."

Aaron was vaguely fascinated at the level of vitriol pouring through the line from two time zones away. "Who's we?"

"Beg your pardon?"

"You said we, Mr."—he glanced down at the Post-it—"Kroll. Who's we?"

"The poets of Delaware. Elia Adank gave a reading in 1992 at the Wilmington Public Library and the drunken buffoon made a remark, I won't even repeat it, but it was extremely insulting to the poets of Delaware, and if he has the nerve, the audacity, the . . . gall to show his stupid face here, he's going to be handed a big fat surprise."

Aaron took a breath. "That sounds like a threat, Mr. Kroll."

"Not a threat, as they say, but a promise."

Aaron glanced down at the breakfast he'd brought in, a croissant with fried egg and a slab of Swiss cheese which, like every other item from the food truck, smelled vaguely of curry. His breakfast had apparently gone cold, as he could no longer detect the microwave-induced steam rising from the half-eaten mass.

As the guy rattled on, the image of Elia Adank manifested in Aaron's head, smiling, then chortling. *Chortling* was a strange word, most often relegated to amateur-level fiction, but Elia Adank was someone who chortled when amused by something from one of the seven languages crowding his brain. Word was that Elia had been a fierce drinker back when he was still delivering readings in English, and Aaron thought it possible—no, quite probable—that pompous, inebriated Elia had insulted his audience, in this case, the poets of Delaware.

Aaron, his breakfast ruined, snatched the dangling thread of mono-logue like a fly buzzing near his head. His curiosity about Leslie Kroll at an end, subtlety and diplomacy were no longer called for.

"You're making this call from Delaware, I assume." Aaron could practically hear gears being shifted on the other end of the line.

"Wilmington is in the state of Delaware. That is correct."

"Look," said Aaron. "I don't know what the laws are. But given that to cross state lines to commit an act of violence is a federal offense, I sus-pect that placing a call across state lines and threatening violence might also be a federal offense. So, I'll tell you what, Mr. Kroll. As soon as we click off, I'm calling the Federal Bureau of Investigation, and I'm going to find out if placing a threatening call across state lines to an institution of higher learning does indeed constitute a federal crime. And whether it does or doesn't, I'm going to ask the FBI to pay you a visit, Mr. Kroll, and at the very least I'm sure you and your ugly face will be placed on a watch list because I believe you're somebody who needs to be watched. I, for instance, will remember your stupid-ass name for as long as I live, and if you ever call up Parami University again and harass our long-suffering administrator or call me directly, I will fuck with your life in ways you've never even dreamed of."

For what Aaron suspected was the first time in a long while, Leslie Kroll had nothing to say. But then Aaron detected something. Laughter. The sonofabitch was laughing at him.

"What's so funny, Mr. Kroll?"

"Ugly," Kroll said. "You called me ugly."

"And why is that so humorous?"

"Well, you've never even seen me, never read my glob, and therefore have no idea what I look like, so why would you call me something like that?"

"You're right, Kroll. I have no idea what you look like. But I'm sure you've posted more than one picture on your glob, so when I get some time, I'll take a peek. If you're not as ugly as you sound, excuse me if I don't call back and apologize."

Aaron hung up the desk phone. He absently picked up the croissant and took a bite. *Curry, why the hell would they put curry into French-style baked goods?* Aaron set the croissant back on its slab of aluminum foil. "The poets of Delaware," he muttered.

CHAPTER 24

Funds and Games

Even though Opal had made a splash with her performance, it was clear that Axis would not be taking her on as an assistant. When Opal went to see her in her office, Axis seemed to only vaguely recall their initial exchange. Opal quickly surmised that Axis had no interest in mentoring anyone who might create anything compelling in the field of Performance, especially a much younger woman. Not only that, Axis, who'd organized the event and urged Opal to participate, hadn't even attended. She did, however, offer what Opal took to be parting words: "If you're still wanting a mentor, keep taking classes with Philip Pristley and say yes when he suggests an Immersive Study."

Opal knew she first got Philip's attention that warm Saturday afternoon in October, when Philip was teaching a weekend practicum in the Timmons Studio. There were twelve students in the class, ten of them women. The class itself wasn't all that interesting to her, Indigenous Inspirations, in which students were urged to look at the photographs and renderings that Philip provided of selected birds and mammals that populated Pearl Handle and its surroundings and compose free-form responses inspired by the images.

Late that morning, Philip had a yellow-billed loon up on the screen when, in apparent distraction or frustration, he looked around the room. The students, scattered on meditation cushions, followed his eyes as they scanned the walls.

"Something's not right," said Philip. "You feel that, don't you?"

No one spoke up, but each set of eyes swept the room, trying to determine what Philip was getting at.

"Here we sit, talking about natural beauty, yet we're cooped up in a classroom."

Alicia Hilliard, one of the Derridas, came out with her annoying, unsettling laugh.

Philip, appearing a bit startled and even more bothered than before, said, "What's funny about that?"

"You said cooped up," giggled Alicia, "and we're studying birds. You know, like a chicken coop."

Philip nodded, as though taking her comment seriously. "Right, well, in a way, that's what I'm referring to. It's gorgeous outside, likely the last day of its kind this season, and we're discussing natural beauty stuck in this sterile environment."

"Let's go outside," said someone.

"Let's hold the class out on Timmons Grove," said someone else.

Philip, seemingly deep in thought, said, "I drove here today, did anyone else?"

A couple of hands went up.

A smile spread over his face. "Why don't we go up to the mountains and see what we can encounter on this exquisite day?"

TWO OTHER VEHICLES followed Philip's Pathfinder up to Sandy Shelf, eighty-five hundred feet above sea level. They'd picked up provisions on the way out of Pearl Handle, and Philip conveniently had a few blankets in his car which they spread out beside tranquil, glistening Bear Face Lake.

After a picnic lunch, instead of trekking off to look for wildlife, Philip suggested that such an idyllic setting should not go to waste.

At his urging, clothes were shed, shrieks pierced the stillness, and, following Philip's lead, the students rushed naked into the water. The only exception was September Riley, a freshman like Opal, who dutifully set out in search of nonhuman creatures to capture on her camera.

The swimming didn't last long, far too cold it was, but when they got out, and everyone shared the towels that Philip had in his car, his eyes kept roving in Opal's direction.

Opal usually wore loose shirts and baggy sweaters and trousers that hung slack from her waist. One of the things she'd done in her life was serve as an artist's model and had been told by more than one fledgling painter that her body itself was a work of art that could never be adequately captured. She made sure Philip got a good long look.

After that day, Philip's eyes would sweep toward her during class like a spotlight, then remain fixed. Opal, seasoned in such matters, knew it was only a matter of time.

The Tuesday before Thanksgiving, the last day of classes for that week, Philip urged her to stay after class for a moment. Waiting until it was just the two of them, he said: "You have some really interesting perceptions, but you keep them to yourself. From what I hear you're a unique and talented performer. I hardly ever initiate this kind of thing with a student, but I'm very curious as to what your next project will be. I know that developing a new creative piece is difficult with all the other demands of your classes. Would you consider doing so as an Immersive Study next semester?"

Opal at once felt weary and invigorated. Weary, because Philip's suggestion was all too predictable; invigorated because she was bored out of her skull and up for an adventure. The bed partners she'd had since coming to Pearl Handle numbered three, which, in terms of carnal interactions, constituted a fallow period for Opal. Two were Parami undergraduate women and the other was an SWU boy who texted her so many times afterward, she had to block him from her phone. Opal hadn't had an older guy since that ship's captain in Athens. Empowered, she asked Philip, "Why wait till next semester?"

"What do you mean?"

"I'm in town over the holiday. Why don't you come over, say, Thanksgiving night?"

THE REVEREND DOCTOR Stamford Moses was driving though drizzling snow, south to Colorado Springs, having been summoned this day before Thanksgiving by Roger Bayne Whitney. That RBW, which is how Stamford had come to think of him, would call for a face-to-face was unusual. Stamford had been in daily contact with the man—emails, texts, calls— sometimes four or five times a day.

Parami was clearly RBW's pet project. Besides updates from Stamford, he was largely concerned with the fiscal aspects, including tuition dollars, grants and donations, holdings and investments, not to mention salaries and expenditures. RBW had probed deep into Parami, determining that the institution, if not solvent, was at least sustainable.

Once they were seated, unlike Stamford's initial visit, RBW got right to the point.

"You know how we've planned to terminate most of the old staff and faculty over the summer? Well, something's arisen, and we're going to need to act on some of those staff positions as soon as the last day of classes before Christmas break." He took a moment: "I'm also going to need to generate a lot of last-minute enrollments from faith-based institutions, calling in favors from all over the country. It's a nightmare."

"What's happened, sir?"

"I've uncovered sixty-six withdrawals from various Parami budgets and accounts."

"How is that possible?"

Clearly wound up, RBW was not in listening mode. "We need to handle this delicately and internally. We're talking in the neighborhood of seven hundred thousand dollars. If it's theft and gets into the press, our new university, everything, will be sunk."

Stamford swallowed through the stone in his throat. "Do you have any idea who's responsible, sir?"

"That Thai woman, Ratana, who's been there forever; if she was going to engage in larceny on this scale, she'd have tried it by now. Trouble is, her accounting system is so chaotic and peculiar, I can't make sense of it. The books are always balanced at the end of each fiscal, but during the academic year, things are strewn all over the place. Since you're on the ground, you need to determine what's going on and whether those funds are missing or just squirreled away somewhere."

THE SNOW HAD turned to a full-on whiteout, yet driving through this winter squall, Stamford was sweating. *This is bad, this is worse than bad.* Roger Bayne Whitney was right about Ratana. Old guard that she was, had she been dipping into the pot, she'd have been found out long ago. *What if it's Madlenka?*

Questions, questions. If they investigated Madlenka, how long would it be until RBW's Essence Center uncovered the affair? What about Delsey, once she found out she'd been betrayed? How harshly would the hand of Roger Bayne Whitney come down on him?

By the time he eased into Pearl Handle, it was the end of the day, but Stamford didn't want to go home. Delsey's sister and her husband had flown in from Chicago and were staying at the house. He didn't feel like putting on the kind of face he'd need to assume throughout the evening; bad enough he had to cohost the feast Delsey had planned for tomorrow's holiday. Stamford was too upset, too on edge. Delsey would surely know something was wrong. Stamford, when forced to lie, had never been adept at it. He texted: *Snow delay Dinner in CS with RBW Home late.*

Stamford drove from one end of Pearl Handle to the other. The snow, done for the day, should have illuminated everything, yet the town appeared gloomy, like there weren't enough streetlights. Almost without realizing it, he found himself parked in the dark in front of Madlenka's duplex.

There were lights downstairs and her car was in the driveway. Stamford sat for a long while, engine running, heat blasting, reluctant to step out into the cold, even more reluctant to knock on the door and confront Madlenka. How to even start? He took a deep breath, then another. His lips moved involuntarily. *Lord, Lord,* were at first the only identifiable words that sputtered out. *I have stumbled, I have fallen. My weakness, my lack of faith. You, who are all good and all knowing, all truth and wisdom . . .*

The front door opened and Madlenka, in a parka with a fur-lined hood, stepped onto the porch, tugging a suitcase as though taking a dog for a walk. Stamford watched her awkwardly trudge down her driveway.

When he opened his door, a chill hit as though it were shoving him back into his car. He hustled toward her, her hatchback open, apparently looking for something, probably a scraper to clear the windshield.

Sensing movement behind her, Madlenka turned. "Stamford, what are you doing here?"

In the past, the sound of her voice would have caused Stamford to smile. But he was in no state to manage a lighthearted response. "Where are you going, Madlenka?"

Abandoning her search, she approached Stamford tentatively.

"On my way to the airport."

"To catch a flight where?"

"Why do you want to know?"

"Where, Maddy?"

Madlenka giggled. "Las Vegas. I have yet to go there, and it sounds like fun."

"I don't think you should go."

"Why shouldn't I? Snow is over." A moment, then: "I need to leave, Stamford. Flight will not wait."

"It's freezing. Let's go inside."

Madlenka sighed. "Only for a minute."

"This is gonna take more than a minute, Maddy."

CHAPTER 25

Leftovers

Aaron ordered Chinese takeout the night before Thanksgiving and only ate half of it. The following day around three o'clock, he heated the other half in the microwave and that was Thanksgiving dinner.

The holiday, he knew, shouldn't matter to him. More than once, during his years in LA, he'd been on his own, including one Thanksgiving at Nate 'n Al's deli in Beverly Hills. But since his accident, he'd felt acutely aware of how isolated he was. Restless, he picked up the book he'd been periodically reading, Lawrence Timmons's *Attaching to Non-attachment*.

Although he'd never tried meditation, he'd been tempted to look into one of the many classes offered at Parami. With the demands of his Seat duties, there was no time to slip one in during the workday and, as soon as the day was over, the last thing he wanted to do was hang around or return for an evening session. This Timmons book did, however, walk the reader through a technique Timmons called Lifting, Lingering, and Leaving.

As instructed, Aaron sat on the edge of the bed, palms on thighs, eyes partially closed and cast downward in a vague, neutral state. Thoughts would come (Lifting), Timmons declared, and one was to watch them as you would a balloon drifting upward in a cloudless sky. At some point the mind would attach itself (Lingering) to the balloon thought and remain with it, for whatever length of time, no matter how trivial or substantial the thought might be, as all thoughts, no matter what their quality, were empty and meaningless. These thoughts would eventually dissipate (Leaving) only to be replaced by another, and the meditating witness would watch it lift, linger, and leave until the time between thoughts dwindled to nothing. Such was the beginning of being able to control the mind and not be controlled by it, the result of which, Timmons was careful to point out, was not emptiness as a destination but the creation of a space where luminosity might manifest.

Aaron's first thought, enclosed like a caption in a comic book, was of Stamford Moses. Some relationships simply didn't spark, and for Aaron, clearly for Moses as well, this was one of them. Moses seemed to disapprove of him. Did Reverend Doctor Moses consider Aaron to be a secular heathen? *What was Moses doing at Parami, anyway? And why would an alternative Eastern-based institution hire a traditional Christian minister?*

That thought dissolved and Aaron thought about Viti. Thank God he had her to hold all those day-to-day details. She seemed much sharper and more capable than, for instance, any of the Arts preceptors. Aaron hoped she'd stay the course, wouldn't quit as so many of the staff at Parami ended up doing, out of frustration and disillusionment. *And what was she forever scribbling in that notebook of hers?*

Then, not an image so much as a feeling came over Aaron. Why had he gotten so upset at that kook who called the office earlier in the week? The guy was obviously pathetic, why had Aaron unloaded on him?

No other thought came behind that, and Aaron was gradually infused with a feeling akin to what he'd experienced after his accident. Pushing against a spreading fear, he roused himself and literally shook off the ominous cloud and an array of invading sensations.

Why the hell was he thinking about this stuff on a holiday? Setting the book aside, he decided to see if the refrigerator was as depleted as when he pulled out the leftover kung pao tofu. *Hmmm.* Still nothing that would constitute a meal or even a substantial serving. He opened the freezer to see if there was any ice cream left. There wasn't, but sticking up in the back, like the exposed hull of a boat buried aground, was the neck of that bottle of Tito's he'd impulsively bought a few weeks back. He yanked it from the teeming ice bin.

Glass in one hand, channel changer in the other, Aaron sat on the couch. Football, NASCAR, sports guys yapping; cooking, jewelry, saleswomen yapping; terrorism, car chase, newspeople yapping; weather, gardening, wildlife; animation, black-and-white western, low-budget horror. All lifting, no lingering.

Aaron hit the off button, then sipped through a second glass of vodka, then a third. A little after seven, already mildly intoxicated, Aaron grabbed his coat with the vague intention to go out drinking.

BY EIGHT THIRTY, Aaron was on a barstool in the Faceless Pub, well into his third—or was it his fourth—glass of Tito's since arriving. The bar was gloomy. Besides Aaron and an athletic-looking male bartender, there was a couple who looked to be in their fifties, a young woman by herself, computer glowing atop the small table in front of her, and three solo men of various ages. The atmosphere was that of a desolate late-night bus ride.

Then he spotted the figure on a stool at the end of the bar, looking as alone as Aaron on this Thanksgiving night, and realized it was none other than Philip Pristley. *What would Timmons do?* "Bartender . . . " The young guy stepped over. "Whatever that man in the corner is drinking, give him one on me."

The bartender gave Aaron a curious glance, then poured a glass of Hennessy's. Setting the drink in front of Pristley, the bartender said something, causing Pristley to peer into the shadows. He didn't recognize Aaron at first, and by the time he appeared to, Aaron was sliding onto the barstool beside him. "These holidays are tough for us bachelors," Aaron said.

Pristley, clearly thrown, said, "You could say that."

"How are your classes going?"

"No complaints."

"Sorry we haven't gotten a chance to talk this semester."

Pristley shifted on his barstool. "We've all been busy, I'm sure."

Aaron took a sip. "No turkey today?"

"No, my . . . the woman I'm . . . went back east to see her family."

Music was dimly playing, some eighties ballad Aaron vaguely recognized.

Pristley tossed back a big gulp, draining his glass. "Well, thanks for the drink, I've gotta be going."

What would Timmons do? "You know, Philip, you and I got off on the wrong foot." Pristley was pulling bills out of his wallet, setting them on the bar. "Never had a chance to talk, except that time last summer in the Plateau, and that wasn't what I'd call a conversation."

Pristley looked at Aaron, for what Aaron realized was the first time. "So, you're apologizing, is that what this is about, buying me a drink and everything?"

Timmons, Timmons, what would Timmons do?

"Why don't we sit in that booth over there? Got a couple questions I'd like to get clear on."

Pristley gave Aaron a sideways glance, then shuffled forward as though taken hostage. Before sitting down, Aaron motioned the bartender for two more drinks, which were swiftly poured and brought over.

Pristley was facing the room, leaning back into the corner of the booth. Aaron sat, his sole perspective being Pristley and the brick wall behind him.

"You been at Parami a long time, right, Philip?"

Pristley nodded.

"Ever take any meditation instruction?"

Another nod. Having never been in close proximity to the man, Aaron took a good look. Pristley's eyes, behind thick lenses, noticeably protruded in what could be taken as a perpetual state of astonishment.

"So, I've been reading Timmons," Aaron pressed on, "his approach toward meditation. I mean, it is interesting to consider what we carry around with us all the time. Some of it's like a junk heap or a hard drive that needs clearing or cleaning."

Pristley took a gulp of cognac.

"Like if I were to meditate now, there'd be thoughts of . . . hell, I don't know, this woman I was seeing back in LA who ended up throwing me over. Or the fact that I'm right-handed and if I ever had to shoot somebody and I was left-handed, I couldn't do it because of an accident I had.

Pristley sat up a little straighter, then let out a harsh laugh. "Are you planning on shooting somebody?"

Aaron laughed himself. "No, not tonight. So, we carry all these experiences around with us and they control us. But wouldn't Timmons say the point is to control them and not let them control *us*? I mean, that *is* the point, isn't it?"

Pristley's expression had gone as frozen as the ice in Aaron's glass. "I need to take a leak, man. Bathroom's in the back, I believe."

Before Aaron could respond, Pristley was scooting out of the booth, leaving Aaron in the blue gloom of the bar.

Five minutes, going on ten. No sign of Pristley.

Aaron got up and walked unsteadily down the tight hallway to the men's room.

One sink, one urinal, no one in sight. Aaron leaned down and couldn't detect anything going on in the single stall.

When he stepped out into the hallway, he noted that the Faceless Pub had a back door, clearly the means through which Philip Pristley had made his departure.

CHAPTER 26

Restraint

Back at his desk the Monday morning after Thanksgiving, Stamford's swarming thoughts kept lighting upon that scene in Madlenka's duplex, the two of them facing each other at the kitchen table, over cooled cups of tea. As Madlenka spoke, laying out her drastic predicament, Stamford felt a cloak of dread spreading around him that had not gone away.

"I need to win to replace what I have borrowed, funds from many corners of the university. Ten thousand here, twenty thousand there, nearly three-quarters of a million dollars. Only a matter of time before Ratana discovers it."

"You can't try to fix it that way, Maddy. It isn't rational."

Madlenka appeared to go colder than the chill out the window. "If you believe in miracles, God-man, you need to help save me from this."

Then she looked into his eyes and, without saying so, told him: *If you do not, you are going down with me.*

"Only hope for me is a discovery I made just today. A Parami account in another bank, Wells Fargo, not Conscious Credit, that seems not to have been touched in more than twenty years."

"Even if that were the case . . . it's not your money, Maddy. You could go to prison over this."

And so could I, Stamford added to himself, for knowing what he knew and not revealing it, for fear of exposing his history with Madlenka.

He'd long suspected that Madlenka had a penchant for addiction, and her addiction to gambling had exploded like one of those hothouse flowers you see blossoming on film. That new passion had put her in the three-quarters-of-a-million hole in which she, and consequently Parami, were woefully dug into.

A knock on his office door startled Stamford back to the present. Kevin stuck his head through the partially opened space. "Sorry to bother you, reverend, but there's a police officer here to see you."

THAT MORNING, AARON returned to campus a little later than usual. Viti was at her desk, writing in her notebook. She closed the book, slid it off to the side, and said, "In the past fifteen minutes, Moses has called three times for you."

"Okay," said Aaron, "I'll call him back."

"No, he wants you to come straight to his office. Some kind of emergency."

When Aaron reached the reception area of the Presider's office, Kevin greeted him gravely. "He's been waiting." He ushered Aaron forward, forgoing his usual offer of chai.

Moses, at his desk, glared at Aaron.

"Good morning, Doctor Moses."

"No, Motherway, it isn't good. Nothing good about it."

Aaron remained standing, waiting for whatever was troubling the Presider.

"I received a visit first thing this morning from the County Sheriff's Office." Moses leaned forward, clutching a document. "The only reason the police aren't still here to serve you directly is that the officer who brought it to campus happens to be a member of my congregation. As a courtesy, he's letting me handle this internally. A blessing, since this kind of thing could easily make its way into the *Pearl Handle Recorder*."

Aaron's head was swimming. "What exactly are we talking about?"

Moses pushed the document closer as though he were prodding Aaron with a stick. "Here, take it."

Aaron grabbed hold of it, then tried to configure the text into something coherent. "What the hell is this?"

"A restraining order, documenting menacing behavior involving the verbal threat of a firearm, apparently under the influence of alcohol, directed by you toward Philip Pristley."

Aaron looked back at Moses.

"You are not to go within three hundred feet of Mr. Pristley, who has identified you as a potential threat to his safety and well-being."

"This entire campus can't be three hundred feet."

"Regina Coyne, at whose home he is living, is identified in this document as well. You are not to approach or speak to her."

"I don't even know her," Aaron uttered.

"You are not to approach, distress, or disturb either of them in any way. It's all spelled out quite explicitly, so you'd better comply." Moses leaned back into his chair. "Speaking frankly, if it weren't the middle of the school year, I'd terminate your interim contract. Parami isn't a playground. An institution like ours should be immune to bullying and intimidation." Eyes probing, he added, "Do you, in fact, possess a firearm?"

"No, and it's probably a good thing right about now." Aaron then walked out, taking his restraining order with him.

THE FOLLOWING WEEK, Aaron was above the library, among the administrative offices. The bathroom in Timmons House only flushed one time out of four and there was no hot water and rarely any hand soap or paper towels. The second floor All Genders Restroom above the library was newer, cleaner, and more likely to be functional.

After doing his business, he stepped out into the hallway to encounter Willa Dickens, a woman in her fifties who'd been Admissions Archon for many years. Her face was flushed, and she'd been crying. "Are you all right?" Aaron asked, knowing she clearly wasn't.

Willa looked at him as though she'd not been aware of his presence. "Oh, I'll be all right," she said, voice fluttering. Then she added: "That is, for somebody who just sold herself out."

There were a couple of armchairs in an open area off the hallway and Aaron said, "Do you want to sit down?"

"No," she said. "I've been told to clean out my desk and that's what I'm about to do." A look crossed her face. "Wait here, there's something you should see."

She was back in a moment, grasping a manila folder teeming with paper.

"Moses made me sign a confidentiality agreement in order to get my severance, but right now I'm so angry I don't care who knows I gave this to you. Moses and company don't know I have them. I copied them before certain elements could be blacked-out or redacted."

She handed the bundle over. As Aaron opened the folder, Willa said, "Not here."

"What is this, Willa?"

She stepped closer. "Transfer students who are coming into the Arts Program starting next semester."

"Next year, you mean? How many are there?"

"Twenty-four, and there'll be here in January, right after break."

Aaron tried to wrap his mind around it. The Arts Program had started the school year with eleven new students, and he was holding evidence that twenty-four had just enrolled, the majority likely leaving other institutions in the middle of the academic year.

"That's a hell of a lot of transfers."

"All from just three different colleges. I can't say any more but sit down with the packet and you'll get the picture."

Aaron took the admissions folder back to his office and closed the door. He opened it and looked down at the completed application on top. He leafed through the document until he came to the letter of intent.

"Though I leave my beloved School of the Covenant, not to mention my beloved Idaho, I understand that coming to Parami is part of the plan my Lord and Savior has devised for me."

He flipped pages until he came to the next student's letter of intent: "Thank you for granting me this opportunity to do the Lord's work. I will dearly miss my outstanding professors as well as my fellow Christian students."

Twenty-four students from only three different faith-based institutions.

Throughout that day, which came to be known as the Christmas Surprise, twenty-seven staffers, mostly those who had been at Parami the longest, were told to clean out their desks, as they were no longer welcome on the property.

CHAPTER 27

Droppings

Presider Doctor Stamford Moses is pleased to announce the addition of Gavin Frenley to our upper staff. Gavin, who comes to us from Liberty, Missouri, will be Director of Marketing and will be assembling a new marketing team. Gavin, fully committed to Mindful Instruction, says: 'I heartily accept the challenge of whipping Parami's brand into focus and putting it forth into the world. This is surely the most vital and gratifying work I can assume at this point in my life and career.' Gavin is the author of *For the Love of Money: Twelve Reasons Why Jesus Wants You to Strike it Rich.*

Following this was a list of the new and newly designated administrative hires, twelve in all. Among their varied accomplishments it was stated that the Assessment and Curricular Objective Specialist, the Overseer of Technology Outreach, and the Student Success Counselor were ordained Christian ministers.

The pervasive nature of these respective backgrounds left no doubt that Moses was drastically and likely permanently transforming Parami. Yet there was no outcry from preceptors or from those still retained on the staff. Aaron knew his days were numbered, even knew what that number was. The restraining order alone guaranteed that his contract, interim or otherwise, would not be renewed, and half the academic year was over already.

Sifting through a pile of mail on his desk, he regarded most of it as junk, primarily promotional materials from textbook publishers. One piece was an envelope with a Florida postmark, addressed to the *Parami Arts Program*. While opening it, Aaron wondered what the people who used to make letter openers had moved on to these days. His aunt—his mother's older sister—had given him a letter opener for his sixteenth birthday. *Whatever happened to it?* She'd also given him a wooden coat hanger for his high school graduation.

There was a letter inside, albeit one intended for collective readership. At the top was a color reproduction of a photograph, taken on a beach, of former Parami Presider Terence Dillard wearing a sagging T-shirt and what looked like a pair of chinos cut off above the knees. His nose was covered with white cream, and he had on a pair of wraparound sunglasses. His wife—*what was her name, Plum, Pear*—was squinting beside him in a floral-patterned, one-piece bathing suit. In the foreground was Dillard's golden lab, a slab of driftwood between its jaws.

> Holiday greetings, be you a Christian, a Jew, a Buddhist, a Hindu, a Muslim, a Sikh, an agnostic, a pagan, or just an old-fashioned honest-to-God atheist. Peach and I and our loyal companion Tigger have had a wondrous several months filled with blessings and relaxation.
>
> Just a year ago, who would have thought that Peach would have taken up genealogy, tracing the fascinating roots of her clan from Connecticut, and that I would have become a blissful bum, strolling on the sand each morning here in Highland Beach and eventually making my way to the Mercy Café (where I'm in fact composing this letter while enjoying my eye-opening double-shot Americano)?

Aaron stopped reading. Had the message been electronic, he would have deleted it, but that it was a letter with an actual stamp on its envelope made it somehow of value. He tossed the rest of the mail in the recycling bin and, without thinking, slid Terence Dillard's Christmas message into the top drawer of his desk.

A scream from the outer office. Shoving back his chair, Aaron got to his feet and yanked open his door only to see Viti dashing out the front.

Aaron stood startled and perplexed. It had been snowing all morning, nine degrees outside, why would she rush out there? He looked around. No trace of anything that would have caused steady, unflappable Viti to run coatless into the elements. The only thing he could assume was that Viti had just received some terrible, life-altering news. Clear that she would not immediately be coming back in, he grabbed his heavy wool coat, wrapped himself in it and went outside.

Viti was standing in the frozen driveway, startled eyes trained upon Timmons House, teeth chattering, tiny clouds of vapor coming from her mouth. Aaron, approaching cautiously, said, "Viti, what's going on?"

"I'm not going back in there."

She appeared deranged. Aaron considered that his assistant was undergoing some long-suppressed psychotic break.

"I'll be working from home today. Go back in there, Aaron, and get me those spreadsheets I just printed out."

"Not until you tell me what happened."

She drew a breath. "I opened my top drawer and a goddamn mouse jumped out onto my lap."

Aaron nodded, recalling a couple of times he'd seen something dark streak across the floor and had written it off to shadows or fatigue. The office was ancient, why wouldn't there be mice in it?

"I'm sorry that happened, Viti. But I'm sure it just got trapped in your desk and is trembling in a hole somewhere."

"No, Aaron, I'm not going back in. Not till you get somebody to do something about it."

"It's freezing out here. C'mon, let's go in together."

But Viti was walking in the direction of the staff parking lot.

AARON WANTED TO go home early that day. Fall Passage was over, he'd turned his grades in, but was convinced if he didn't take action on the rodent front, he wouldn't be seeing Viti after the holidays.

He called Mitchell Amritt's extension at Grounds and Facilities. Aaron had never had a conversation with Mitchell, just a nodding acquaintance, but was aware of Mitchell's history, having been the moonlighting sex worker responsible for the collapse of nationally known evangelist Thaddeus Fogarty.

Aaron asked him to come over, and Mitchell showed up ten minutes later. As he stepped into the office and took off his wool stocking cap, Aaron noted subtle lines on Mitchell's otherwise youthful face. Mitchell's infamous line of work had to be a young man's game. Yet knowing Parami's salaries, Aaron wondered if Mitchell ever went back to it during the midnight hours.

"What can I do for you, Aaron?"

"It seems that here in Timmons House we have a bit of a rodent issue."

"Rats or mice?"

Aaron felt a bit startled, having not considered the much more distressing former possibility.

"Mice."

"And you're just catching on that you have them?"

"I've never seen much evidence—residue, or anything."

"That's because the undocumented cleaning crew, who don't speak English and who most of the day-timers never see, come in at night and remove the droppings."

"They're pests, why doesn't somebody get rid of them?"

Mitchell smiled like he was instructing some clueless pupil. "This is, like it says in the promo, a compassion-based institution. Lionel, who heads Facilities, is a long-term Timmons disciple and won't let us so much as swat a fly. Doesn't want the karma." Mitchell's face brightened even further. "Why do you think you've got a couple hundred prairie dogs in your yard? The Chamber won't do anything because Lionel has convinced them the critters were here first and shouldn't be displaced from their home." Mitchell pulled out a vape pen. "You mind?"

Mitchell took his first puff, igniting the fake blue flame.

Aaron said, "Mice carry hantavirus. Do you think you could take on a project over semester break?"

Mitchell exhaled a pale cloud of vapor. "Get rid of your mice?"

"Precisely."

"If you catch them and turn them loose, they'll just come back. And I'm not an exterminator, you'll have to hire one."

"I don't want to bring anybody in," said Aaron. "I've got some money in the budget for contract labor. I'll say it's for furniture renovation, something like that. It can all be done after hours. Just make sure the cleaning crew isn't around."

Mitchell took another drag, clearly weighing the issue. "I could get canned for that, although the way things have been going, I'll probably get canned anyway."

"Nobody needs to know. Look, I'm afraid if this doesn't get taken care of over break, I'll lose my administrator."

Mitchell looked around like he was searching for a place to extinguish his fake cigarette. Then he said: "Okay, you're on. I can't say anything about the rest of the campus but . . . " He smiled. "By the night before Christmas, all through Timmons House, not a creature will be stirring, especially not a fucking mouse."

CHAPTER 28

Break

Stamford's purification project had started with his office, then the building in which it was situated. He'd cleaned out the closets and nooks. The false idols he'd unearthed were, to him, decidedly unsettling. Once he'd gotten rid of those dusty and spiritually corroded items, he set about cleansing the very air. Each Thursday and Friday evening of Christmas break, Stamford would, usually accompanied by a carefully selected colleague of faith, slip into one of the structures—an administrative office, a classroom—and dispense incense and sprinkle water RBW said came all the way from the River Jordan. *Who knew what arcane, unspeakable abominations had taken place in this citadel of license and confusion?*

The Thursday evening before Christmas, Stamford had with him Tad Darlington, who'd just arrived from a ministry in South Carolina to be Parami's Comptroller, a newly created position. Stamford was clutching an oversize ring of keys, identical looking, save for a tiny number on one side, having identified in advance the one that opened the side door of Timmons House.

The door creaked open into a spacious conference room. Oh, how Stamford hated to think about the vile abominations that had gone on around that table. The light was harsh, consisting of a pair of bare bulbs, exposed wires dangled from the ceiling. Stamford shed his heavy overcoat and carefully placed it on the massive conference table. Over his suit, he wore a velvet sash.

"You can almost taste the evil," whispered Darlington, his demeanor that of one who'd stepped into a cave and come upon remnants of a Black Mass.

Stamford pulled out the missal in his breast pocket, a gift from a Catholic priest.

While Stamford didn't care much for papists, he fervently believed in the existence of Satan and the reality of evil. Catholics did seem to have devised effective rituals to combat demonic forces. The first time Stamford had palpably faced evil was at a meth house in Iowa, experiencing the same feeling that would sometimes overcome him at Parami.

Darlington was carrying a chalice wrapped in a baby blanket. When filled with incense and lit, its attached chains would be gently swung and its ignited coals would purify the spiritually fetid molecules in the room.

Stamford opened his missal to its marked page, then stopped cold. "Hold on a second, brother. What is that contraption in the corner?" Stamford stepped over and looked down. He considered crouching to better observe the object, but the garish strip on top rendered it unnecessary: Caution, Electronic Trap. And in smaller letters: Mouse and Rat Catcher.

Stamford knew that in Parami's humanist belief system, even the earth's vermin—snakes, insects, rodents—were allowed to thrive. Yet this was no humane trap, designed to capture mice for subsequent release. This was a mini electric chair; a mouse would enter, enticed by the bait, only to be zapped into extinction. Even in this den of pestilence, Stamford couldn't help but feel pleased that he'd stumbled upon something he could add to the institutional offenses he was compiling against Aaron Motherway.

NEW YEAR'S EVE, Daniel Coyne was in his suite at the Raphael in downtown Pearl Handle. He'd decided to check in there for the holidays and break his mind-numbing routine at the condo, but the return wasn't having the effect he'd hoped for. Stretched out on the bed, a metal tray balanced across his lap, Daniel was listlessly pushing around a slab of meat loaf and a mound of mashed potatoes, a wordless prayer whispering within him. His prayers, fervent and frequent, were always about him and Regina patching up their ruptured union.

Were that miracle to happen, given that Daniel was now a Christian, he would insist that Regina commit herself to the Lord as well. But that vow would, like Daniel's, need to be held in secrecy. Roger Bayne Whitney had insisted on Daniel being a covert soldier. This didn't mean that Daniel's beliefs were any less ardent than any other who had committed themselves to Faith.

"You just need to keep in the shadows, like a spy, a spy for Truth. Most importantly, that means remaining on the board of trustees at Parami, making certain our plans remain steadfast and sure."

It wasn't easy, attending those trustee meetings. They weren't frequent but were endless, as Parami protocol meant that everyone had to be heard from, no matter how ponderous or pointless their monologue.

Daniel could see clearly what he had previously not perceived: that the Timmons Trustees were lost souls, sheep wandering endlessly, enamored of whatever sounds they were capable of making, roaming through a confused mass of clouded darkness, expending the precious lives that God had given them.

Daniel prayed that Regina would not continue on the Parami path. Yes, he longed to be with her, her body beside him at night, eyes lighting up behind her lenses when he entered a room, her laughter over a cup of morning coffee. He wanted to be buried beside her as they'd planned, for death would be but a brief interruption, leading to their eternal union in the Lord's heaven. If Daniel couldn't save her soul, she needed to save herself, break free of that demon Pristley.

That was why, on this seemingly mundane evening, at exactly 8:10, Daniel Coyne, whose life had been shattered and shredded, received the answer to his one prayer. A ding from his phone, beside him on the table in his well-appointed yet dismal room in the Raphael. The text beamed like a message from paradise itself: *in trrible shape plse come*

Daniel frantically got dressed and took the stairs—*what if the elevator stalled*—down to the parking garage. He lunged into his trusty Lexus and gunned it the mile and a half to the house.

When he approached the front door, it swung open, and he was surprised to see Ula, whose housekeeping duties usually ended at five thirty, standing in the doorway.

"Your lady is upstairs," she declared.

Daniel swung by her and took the steps two at a time, veering left down the shadowed hall that led to the master bedroom.

Regina was curled up on top of the covers, wearing what looked to Daniel like one of many white, heavily starched dress shirts he'd left behind, and little or nothing else. Her hands folded in front of her face, she was whimpering. Daniel's mind lurched back to a previous Christmas season, early in their courtship, when they were skiing in Aspen. Regina narrowly missed a tree but had tumbled, dislocating her knee cap. Daniel recalled feeling a bit guilty that it felt good to have Regina rely on him so acutely, as he relished taking care of her.

And now that face he loved more than any other, tearstained and trembling, turned to him from the bed so tainted by her coupling with Philip Pristley.

"That lowlife asshole took what he could, then cheated on me." She dove into Daniel's chest and sobbed. "Just like you said he would, my dearest. Just like you said."

CHAPTER 29

Troops

During break, Aaron didn't travel, didn't even go out much. The down time made him aware of how busy he'd been throughout Fall Passage. As the resumption of school approached, he found himself almost looking forward to the feverish demands of teaching and running the program. The only time he went to the office was to go in and, with Mitchell, remove the mousetraps the Sunday evening before Acclimation week. Without offering any details, Aaron assured Viti that Timmons House was now rodent free and there would be no more surprises leaping out of her top drawer and onto her lap.

Synod, the formal kickoff to the second semester, was scheduled at noontime, the first day of classes. As Viti had explained to Aaron, each department or program was to be represented by offering and then expounding upon a quote from Lawrence Timmons's recorded talks or a passage from his published writings.

In recent years the Arts Program had not participated. This year, the newly configured Chamber of Wisdoms was insisting that every discipline contribute, so it fell to Aaron to provide the Arts perspective.

For Aaron's presentation, he chose a story that Lawrence Timmons recorded titled "When a Burglar Enters a Temple, All He Sees Is What's

Shining." The meaning of this, which Aaron intended to capsulize, was that one's foremost worldly desires governed how one perceived the world. If you were materialistic, you would see everything in terms of financial and physical comfort. For gluttons it was food; for the lust-filled, sex; for the fame-hungry, ego fulfillment.

The Thursday of Acclimation week, Aaron went to the front desk of Timmons Library and asked for a DVD of the Parami Synod from the previous spring. Then he went back to his office and slipped the disc into his computer. He scanned forward to locate the part of the program where Presider Dillard delivered his beginning-of-Passage address. On his way to that point, Aaron came upon the image of Katryn Burley, autoharp at her shoulder, and Aaron impulsively hit pause, then play.

Buddha was a cowboy,
He rode an ageless horse.
Buddha was a cowboy who kept a steadfast course.
He knew we come from nothing but strove to find the
source.

Aaron hit fast-forward and caught the speeded-up image of Terence Dillard stepping up to the podium.

"Knowing that I was going to be speaking to you today, I began to think long and hard about what I was going to say." Dillard glanced up from his notes. "Well, thinking hard like that, you can imagine what I came up with." He chuckled. "A big fat nothing." He dramatically lifted his script and dropped it to the floor. "How on earth can nothing be big and fat? Nothing is nothing, right? Emptiness. So, then I did what so many of you do—being more advanced practitioners than I—when you sit in meditation. I thought of nothing, and out of that space, that blank page, atoms began to manifest and lift, and I found them chaotic and confusing, and as they lingered, I sensed that, while each contained some kernel of information, they only served to make me more confused. But then, out of this swarm, this chaotic mass, a luminous phrase took shape, and what it said was: "The devil is in the details, but so are the angels."

Aaron kept watching and listening as Dillard took that phrase as a springboard to launch into a new fundraising initiative, as well as plans for the future of Parami. This was a no-limits wish list, what the universe might manifest if the university would only have the faith and courage to envision expanding into a bigger campus that included student dormitories and preceptor housing and a student union; a fitness center, a meditation hall where students and staff and preceptors could renew themselves between classes. There would be even more emphasis on Mindful Instruction, for that was Parami's special gift to the field of education; bringing in high-profile guest lecturers on contemplative topics that would be streamed on the World Wide Web.

Aaron watched with a growing sense that the things Dillard was unpacking, varied though they were, had one element in common. They were long term. And then a question formulated: Why would someone who'd presented a list of such goals announce his retirement six months later?

The man had obviously made a deal.

Then Aaron wondered: Was that deal in place when Dillard invited Aaron to head up the Arts Program. And if it were: Why would he do that?

STAMFORD HAD TO accept the challenge of integrating the substantial influx of students into Parami. First, he worked with the newly appointed Registrar, whom he'd brought in from a small bible institute in Louisiana, and made sure that those students, insofar as possible, were siloed in classes taught by faith-based instructors. Having no dorms and no student union, Parami afforded students little opportunity to congregate.

Such a substantial influx could be managed, he felt, as long as they remained mum regarding their purpose.

Reverend Doctor Stamford Moses's covert Synod began at midnight in Parami's Plateau Performance Space. Taking a cue from RBW, he considered the congregation of fresh-faced students assembled before him as Troops. For their willingness to participate in the Parami takeover, many of them had been promised, upon graduation, teaching jobs at faith-based institutions, or scholarships to divinity programs. Stamford felt it was imperative to welcome them with a hearty endorsement of their mission.

"You have assumed a challenge," the reverend doctor told them. "There is a cultural war we have long been engaged in. You have signed up for this, a gesture that is profoundly appreciated and will not go unnoticed or unrewarded either in this life or the eternal life to come.

"You have placed yourselves at ground zero for this battle. You will find yourselves surrounded by persons approximately your age who might seem harmless, sweet, even seductive. Do not be fooled. That sweetness is bitter. That sweetness has the capacity to snag and snare and pull you down. You will find yourself entangled like them in a thicket of confusion from which it will not be so easy to get free. They may seem like you, they may look like you, but believe me, they are not. They were not raised in pious and loving households as you were. Many of these misguided young souls had hippie parents; they come from fractured homes where many of those parents engaged in relations with multiple partners, where alcohol and drugs were daily aberrations.

"You need to seem open to them and, with the guidance of your teachers, if you see a genuine opportunity to bring them over to our side, you have an obligation to do so. But our plan can never be obvious, it must remain secret. There will come a time when this institution, this battlefield, will be ours. But that victory will not be immediate. That victory will be guaranteed when the number of the faithful has tipped the divine scales and everyone left standing on this patch of smoldering earth will say, 'What happened here, what took place? This used to be Satan's laboratory and now it belongs to our Lord and Master.'

"A final point. It is essential that you attend every one of your classes, and that you arrive on time. I have instituted a new policy that two unexcused absences or three lates will result in expulsion. Knowing the lax attendance embedded in this institution, this mandate will ensure a rapid and resounding cleansing of the student body. So, make certain you show up for every session in its entirety. Are you ready to commence your mission?"

And, as it was late and the campus was dark, the doors shut tight, two hundred eighteen young and vigorous voices thundered their commitment.

CHAPTER 30

Citrus Intolerant

The office of the Presider is pleased to announce a higher-than-average number of transfer students this semester. This happy circumstance is the result of a gold star effort by Parami's redesigned Marketing Department, which inaugurated a short-term but intensive campaign that included outreach to spiritually based institutions, seeing if there was interest among them to study a different spiritual discipline in order to identify the sameness and like-mindedness therein. We are pleased to say that effort was a rousing success as there is eagerness among these students to explore Mindfulness instruction to see what common ground might bind us.

While Aaron was aware that there were two dozen new students in the Arts Program, none of them were enrolled in his two classes. And while he had a cursory acquaintance with Randall Hendricks, he had yet to meet Frances Thrush, having only glimpsed her from a distance. After combing through the email, he decided to do something he'd been doing periodically, check in on Leslie Kroll's glob.

He was greeted with an unflattering head shot of the poet in a red stocking cap covering what Aaron assumed to be a bald pate. Fleshy face dotted with gray stubble and a grape-sized mole to the left of his chin. Kroll had a smile that didn't make it up to his eyes.

The night of January 28 is nearly upon us! Write it down in your calendar, emblazon it in your mind and memory, for on that night, Elia Adank brazenly returns to Wilmington for the first time since his odious appearance on May 17, 1992. On that occasion, Adank—a minor poet then, and still a minor poet—made a remark that stung the minds and hearts of all in the Delaware Poetry Community. Asked why our Delaware Poets had not received more translations into other languages, the chuckling, self-indulgent Adank stated: "Because the work I've seen from this region must first be composed in acceptable English." Some even laughed, can you imagine? Be assured that This Poet did not, and all these years has followed the modest publications and audio offerings of Mr. Adank, hoping the man would have the courage to return here to be confronted by The Poets of Delaware. That day has arrived, Fellow Delaware Poets: Elia Adank is coming! While he could (and perhaps should) be met with stale cabbages and rotten apples to be hurled at that smug, self-gratified, Germanic face, this Delaware Poet urges that Adank be met with absence and silence.

Viti stepped into Aaron's office. He took his eyes off the computer screen. "What's going on?"

"A student just walked in, September Riley. It looks like the Registrar assigned her to Philip Pristley's seminar, and she wants to be placed in another class."

"What's the reason for that?"

"Remember Philip's weekend practicum, last fall? According to September, it was supposed to be in Timmons Studio, but are you aware of where it was conducted?"

Aaron shook his head.

"He took the entire class up to Bear Face Lake for a nude picnic followed by a couple of hours of skinny-dipping. She has pictures on her phone, Philip surrounded by a half-dozen bare-breasted female students, all of them waist deep in water."

Aaron sighed involuntarily, as Viti continued. "September refused to take her clothes off and go in the water and spent the entire afternoon stuck at nine thousand feet. To make matters worse, Philip gave her an Incomplete while he gave the rest of the class As. One of whom, September wouldn't say who, is now having a romantic relationship with Philip."

Aaron took a moment. Moses had made it clear that his newly appointed Registrar was assigning students to classes. The only other lit seminar, with one seat available, was being taught by Frances Thrush. Aaron didn't feel like running to the Registrar or to Academic Engagement or to Moses himself to ask permission for something that should have been Aaron's call in the first place. If Pristley had betrayed Parami's most valued trustee, the Presider would be made aware of it soon enough. Besides, Moses hadn't listened when Aaron urged him to close the Immersive Study loophole. "Tell September," Aaron said to Viti, "I'll see to it she's placed in a different seminar."

LATER THAT DAY, bright and unaccountably warm, Aaron stood at the food truck reacquainting himself with the menu, a kind of living document, elements emerging and receding with each visit. He considered the Mediterranean salad but recalled the one time he'd ordered it, lettuce sprinkled with crumbs of feta and a few non-pitted olives. Then he thought about the Taste of Italy, but he'd had it before, rice pasta with tomato sauce and a few flakes of parmesan. Open Border was rice and beans and a dash of Tabasco. Kung pao vegetables, rice with onions and a few peanuts. Ganges Delight, spinach and cauliflower, thinly coated in cheese sauce.

Tantra, the edgy, emaciated guy who captained the food truck, was assisted by student employees who shifted as often as the menu. "What'll it be, my brother?" asked Tantra, when it was Aaron's turn to order.

"What kind of sandwiches do you have?"

"Egg salad, chicken salad, tuna salad. For a dollar fifty more, each of them comes with a bag of chips."

"What kind of chips?"

"Barbeque, jalapeno, or regular with sea salt."

"How much are the chips without a sandwich?"

"A dollar fifty."

"I see. Just the sandwich, please."

"What kind?"

"Oh, sorry. Is the tuna fresh?"

Tantra glared. "I didn't yank it out of the ocean, but I think it would pass the smell test."

"Okay, then. On whole wheat, not toasted, with whatever you put on it."

"It's tuna with mayonnaise and chunks of celery. We humans can only distinguish three different flavors at any given time."

"Where did you hear that?"

"It's a fact. Culinary experts all over the world will bear me out."

"Could I also have some orange juice?"

"No orange juice anymore. A kid was in line during Acclimation, and when I opened a carton of orange juice for somebody else, he started gagging and his eyes teared up and he ran straight to the Disability Coordinator. No more orange juice, man."

"Because one student out of the entire school had a bad reaction, no one gets any orange juice?"

"No grapefruit juice either. Nothing that would affect anybody who's citrus intolerant. They didn't say anything about lemonade, and I do have some of that. You still want the sandwich?"

Aaron sat at a nearby picnic table. The tuna sandwich tasted faintly of curry; the cup of lemonade, vaguely of chai. The picnic table he was sitting at seated six, and Aaron became aware that the bench facing him was occupied. "Hello, Betsy."

Aaron hadn't interacted with Betsy Cohn since the day she and Feldman and Jordy Hurwitz had come to see him in his office.

"I have a bone to pick with you," she said.

Aaron set down his curry-tainted sandwich.

"Rahsaan Jerome Cooke."

"What about him?"

Betsy leaned forward. "The man promotes violence and cultural divisiveness. Not to mention he has six different children from four different women."

Aaron looked back at her.

"Rahsaan Jerome Cooke is one of the foremost contemporary poets. I'd be doing a disservice to our students, especially our writing students, to not expose them to a singular and provocative poetic voice."

Had he an apple, Aaron thought, he'd have tossed it on the ground just to see Betsy come unglued.

CHAPTER 31

Immersive Study

The newly formed Sadistic Treatment of Pollock (STOP) has determined that pets are no longer welcome in Parami classrooms. While some may assume that objections to pets came from Parami students or preceptors, the organization wants it understood that this decision is more out of concern for the pets themselves. In a classroom setting, nonverbal beings (primarily dogs and sometimes cats) become bored and restless in what for them can prove to be a confined and oppressive environment.

At his desk, Aaron picked up the phone and dialed Missy Samuels, the newly hired Student Success Counselor, the designated go-to person regarding a student in crisis.

"This is Missy," she answered, in a cheery voice.

"Aaron Motherway, over at the Arts Program. I have a student, Nolan Pickering, who I'm concerned about."

"The undergraduate male who came to us from Virginia? You're not the first instructor who's called."

"I haven't seen him the last two class sessions, and I'm a little worried. I did leave him a message to come in at two this afternoon, but I'm not holding out a lot of hope. Do you know if he's still in town or gone back to Virginia, or what?"

"I'll ask you what I asked his other preceptors. Are you familiar with the new university attendance policy?" Her cheery tone had noticeably receded.

"I saw the email about it. Two unexcused absences means failure?"

"That is correct. And this student, this . . . Pickering boy, has missed two or more sessions in every course he's enrolled in. Unlike the previous policy, where failing a semester would result in academic probation, now it means a total washout."

"I know what you're saying, but—"

"Parami's tendency has been to coddle such students in the past, but what we're talking about here is a lost cause. It's going to be a lot more efficient to help the students win who want to be winners, not the Nolan Pickerings of the world."

"Are you aware of what Nolan is dealing with?"

"Well aware. And while I applaud your compassion, Mr. Motherway, the fact is that since the Pickering boy has failed your class as well as all of his others, he's effectively no longer a student, so we shouldn't even be talking about him."

"Did I dial the wrong number? You only help students who *aren't* in trouble?"

"As I said, Nolan Pickering is no longer a student."

Aaron slammed down the phone. He sat there a moment, pleased he had a landline. With a cell phone, you could click off but not really slam the phone down on someone as annoying as Parami's Student Success Counselor.

AARON WAS IN his office when, at 2:00 p.m. exactly, Nolan Pickering showed up in his scarlet bathrobe. Masking his surprise at seeing him, Aaron motioned for the young man to take a chair, as he still considered Nolan Pickering an enrolled, tuition-paying student.

"Nolan, we need to talk about your spotty attendance, your lack of engagement." The fumes from the bathrobe had infused the air in the ever-tightening space. "As well as a few other, ah, pressing issues."

Nolan gazed at Aaron. His expression was not hostile or defensive but exuded a kind of wonder.

Aaron pressed on. "The first thing you have to do is lose the bathrobe. I know you feel you're making a statement, but frankly the other students are getting uncomfortable." All but gagging, Aaron added, "I'm pretty uncomfortable myself."

An amused expression registered at each corner of Nolan's mouth, but still, no audible response.

"So, I'm willing to go to bat for you, but if you have any hope of passing, you're going to need to attend every class, take part in the discussions, and you and the bathrobe are going to have to part company."

Nolan blinked a few times as though he were trying to wordlessly communicate.

"I know there's no dress code, but the classrooms don't have all that much ventilation," Aaron sputtered like some kind of mechanical device running down. Stillness in the room until Aaron said, "For god's sake, Nolan, say something."

Nolan smiled and reached into the pocket of the bathrobe and pulled out a scrap of paper. Smile frozen, he handed the paper to Aaron.

Like Lawrence Timmons, I am now silent.

Nolan appeared vacant and at the same time brimming with unnamable emotion.

"Let me ask you something, Nolan. How the hell are you going to complete the semester if you're quite capable of talking but simply choose not to? You may have noticed that participation in critiques and discussions is one of the major elements of our workshop."

Nolan held his left palm out and, above it, made a fluttering motion with his other hand. It took a moment for Aaron to realize the kid wanted to write something down. Aaron picked up a pad of paper and a pen off his desk and handed both to Nolan.

A few seconds, then the pad and pen were handed back.

Quitting school.

OPAL AND PHILIP were in her gloomy, first floor apartment. It was dawn and they'd been up all night. She was clad in only a thong, and he was in his briefs and moccasins. Spread out on a coffee table were miniature statues, some wooden, some plastic, purchased from Eastern-themed shops on Pearl Handle's Middle Street mall, as well as Christian-themed storefronts in Denver. In a ceramic bowl were globs of tomato paste mixed with red dye, glue and V8 juice. Both Opal and Philip were clutching thin brushes.

"It's getting light outside," said Philip, his voice dry and weary. "I thought we might go to bed at some point. Maybe mess around a bit before going to sleep."

Opal did not look up from the statue of Saint Peter, which she was tainting with red goo. "Why are you so fixated on that? You know what Warhol said: 'Sex is the biggest nothing there ever was. Get famous and you can have whoever you want.'"

"I don't know why you committed to having this done so quickly. I think there's more to making an installation than you're counting on."

Opal set the statue aside, then reached for a fresh one. "How is it any different than throwing a party? My parents throw parties all the time. Big ones. And they always come off. In this case, you're just asking people to come to look at something."

"Well," said Philip. "I've never done anything like this, and you haven't either."

Opal set the half-brushed figure down on the table. "Wait a minute, I'm getting an idea."

Philip set the figure he was holding beside hers. Opal's ideas were usually implausible, and she had them all the time. He looked at her with what he hoped would be taken as interest.

Opal was pacing, something she shifted into as creativity set her alight. "The concept is depictions of all kinds of religious icons covered in what Opal is claiming is blood. Guaranteed to push a lot of buttons, right? But what if Opal were to make it exclusive?"

"I'm not following."

"What if we . . . *Opal*, invited an audience . . . at random? At least that's what Opal says she's doing. You can bet that a lot of uninvited people will still want to come or will be talking about it. Only Opal won't invite anyone, will not show anyone anything, will just describe it and let them picture in their own minds what they think the show is." Opal beamed, just short of clapping her palms in delight. "It's the ultimate concept."

CHAPTER 32

Accounts

Stamford knew it was wrong, but knew he had to do it. If, as Madlenka claimed, there was a forgotten account, he needed to recover it, so that she could spread the funds over the holes she'd created throughout Parami's fiscal terrain. Phone to his ear, watery vibrations that were supposed to pass for music coming from the other end, Stamford was holding for the branch manager of the Wells Fargo in midtown Pearl Handle.

A voice crackled: "Shelby Quarten, how may I help you?"

"Doctor Stamford Moses, Parami University. I'm calling about an account we have at your bank."

"I figured this day would come."

Stamford sat a little higher in his chair.

The branch manager chuckled. "We always wondered why your institution would let such a substantial sum just sit there."

Stamford took a beat. "How much is in the account . . . at present, that is?"

"Last I looked it was around eight twenty-five."

Feeling his jaw drop, Stamford said, "That's *thousands* we're talking about?"

"Yep, eight hundred twenty-five of them."

A deep breath, then: "We've been waiting for the right moment to apply those funds and I feel we've at last reached it."

"Let's see here. The initial certificate of deposit was in one of our California branches for five hundred twenty-five thousand, then wire-transferred here. This was back in September '94. The rates were substantially higher in those bygone decades. But you've accrued, let's see, a little over three hundred thousand since then. Three names on the account, but all correspondence, statements, and the like, have been bouncing back for going on fifteen years. My understanding is, it was a consortium of three different rock bands, based in California. We've given up on the three individuals who inaugurated the account. My guess is they're dead or have forgotten about it entirely. Each band, I believe, broke up years ago. Says here, 'Arts Repository funds are to be used for the purchase of state-of-the-art equipment, plus a full-time archivist, plus part-time staff, to establish and maintain the production and preservation of texts, audiotapes, videotapes, and related materials.'"

Stamford struggled to maintain his composure. "Well, the time has come for those funds to be activated."

A moment. "That might be tricky."

Stamford took a moment as well. "And why would that be?"

"It stipulates that the funds are to be used for their stated purpose. I'm sure you're familiar with that issue regarding institutional gifts. We deal with it all the time with SWU. Donors want to make sure the monies will be applied as offered. In this case, it's stated that only Willard Pettibone can withdraw funds in order to put them to use."

"Mr. Pettibone is deceased."

"We're aware of that, saw it in the *Recorder* a few years back."

Empty air, then something stirred in Stamford. "Since Willard Pettibone was founder of the Parami Arts Program, wouldn't responsibility for those funds be assumed by his duly appointed successor?"

LESLIE KROLL SAT in his pickup truck in the frigid evening darkness outside Wilmington's Banks Gallery. He had no intention of going in there for Elia Adank's reading, and those who did come—well, he couldn't be responsible if they'd been so impudent as to not heed his message. The heat in the truck's cab wasn't sufficient. He cranked it up higher and, with his Bic lighter, relit his White Owl cigar, which had gone cold. He was going to enjoy the cigar until it was time to put it to its other use.

Leslie estimated around twenty people in scattered attendance, along with a front row of reserved empty chairs.

Here come some people now—six, no, eight of them. In the light spilling from the gallery onto the sidewalk, Leslie made out the fetid presence of Adank himself who, like the other fools, was likely fresh from an expensive meal that included fine wine and elegant desserts. Well, Leslie had drunk some wine himself, albeit not as aged and refined as what had passed the lips of that pretentious cow, Elia Adank.

The animated group was going in now, all aflutter with their scarves and gloves and heavy coats.

The action would be swift and precise, leaning down and lifting the gasoline-filled wine bottle, neck stuffed with a rag, then stepping out and touching the glowing tip of his cigar to the cloth. Once it was ignited, he would hurl the bottle through the window, turning Elia Adank's despicable reading into mayhem.

Someone was at the lectern now, a woman Leslie did not recognize, and although Leslie couldn't hear it, he knew she was introducing Adank, checking off the list of undeserved awards and meaningless publications. The small gathering was soundlessly putting their hands together, and red-faced, huffing Elia Adank was making his way to the front, smiling and curiously shifting his arms as though clearing unseen objects out of his way.

Now he was poised at the lectern, no microphone in front of him, the tight ambience and the gallery's high ceiling apparently enough for Adank's sickening voice to carry.

Adank would be up there for a half hour, forty minutes, but why wait? The tableau was not going to change. All Leslie had to do was grab hold of his missile, ignite its fuse, and fling it with all the fury that had, for years, been simmering within him.

Leslie reached down and across, then pulled the bottle up to his lap. About to push open the door and step out onto the street, Leslie froze.

His cigar had gone out again.

What he'd envisioned as a seamless action was like a moving picture put on pause. This was not how he'd planned it, having to relight his cigar. Still, he opened the door and stepped out. He crouched, concealing himself as much as possible from any sight lines from the gallery. He tossed the cigar onto the pavement and switched the wine bottle into his left hand. With his right hand, he reached into the outer pocket of his overcoat and pulled out the lighter. He flicked the tiny cylinder and . . . a spark, just a spark. Again, a spark, not enough to light the rag. Another and another . . . A disaster. No time to go purchase another lighter or get his hands on a pack of matches. With his thumb he flicked the cylinder as forcefully as he could, but the sparks kept getting smaller, then disappeared altogether. Furious, Leslie flung the lighter aside.

He stood there a moment, then yanked the useless rag from the bottle, dropped it on the pavement and poured out the gasoline. He thought about tossing the empty bottle through the window, the glass startling Adank, putting a stop to his damnable reading, but that would fall short of what had been a glorious plan.

Feeling helpless and useless, Leslie climbed back into his pickup, shoved the gearshift from neutral into first and, having failed to achieve vengeance for the Poets of Delaware, pulled away.

CHAPTER 33

Restorations

Utmost Importance! Richard Eaves, Preceptor of World Wisdoms, who previously brought to the university's attention that the cushions in Timmons Meditation Hall all have dimensions not accommodating to him, has registered a new request. Richard, who self-identifies as a Person of Size, says that the special cushion he was provided with, while dimensionally acceptable, sets him apart from the other Meditators, resulting in an unwanted sense of self-consciousness. Therefore, Richard is requesting that all meditation cushions be expanded to match his. This pressing issue will be taken up at the next . . .

Aaron's landline jingled. Seeing the logo on the caller ID, he collected himself before lifting the receiver. "Arts Program," he said.

Every other time the Presider's office had phoned, he was met with the voice of Kevin, Moses's Protocol Facilitator. But this time, it was the Presider himself. After a couple of empty preliminaries, Moses said: "It's a lovely day. Let's you and I go for a walk, shall we?"

THE PEARL HANDLE RIVER bordered the south end of the Parami campus. As Moses approached, Aaron stood waiting in a tight patch of ground beside the rushing water. Betsy Cohn had continued grumbling about Rahsaan Cooke's reading, threatening to organize a protest even, and Aaron figured he was about to get an earful, maybe even be terminated because of it.

Aaron fell into step, and neither man said anything as they strolled along the riverbank. The wind had kicked up, and Moses's hands were thrust into the pockets of a suede jacket, more casual than Aaron was accustomed to seeing him. Aaron had on a thick wool sweater that buttoned up the front, leather patches on each elbow. He thought of this sweater as academic drag. The ground was damp, and he wished he was wearing boots instead of the loafers he'd selected that morning, not anticipating that the day would include a constitutional with Parami's Presider.

Moses's voice, resonant and even, came from beside Aaron.

"You and I haven't had the occasion to share anything meaningful on a personal basis, have we, Aaron?"

"Not really, doctor."

"You must be noticing some institutional changes of late."

Aaron didn't respond, just kept up the deliberate pace.

Moses continued, "I see it as a broadening of perspective, keeping what's sound and effective, as well as introducing elements that I feel will help Parami be fully dimensional, better positioned to take part in the global educational and spiritual conversation."

Not knowing where this was going, Aaron remained in step.

"It's an enormous challenge to maintain Parami's uniqueness yet take it in entirely fresh and even more inclusive directions. The arts have always been vital to Parami's mission and legacy, and I want to make sure those elements are preserved. Are you aware that the entire history of the program, from Willard Pettibone to the present, is warehoused out east of town? We need to start addressing those materials, as it's my understanding that many of them are on cassettes and reel-to-reel tapes, which have been deteriorating with every year they sit there. In going through Mr. Pettibone's effects, we discovered there was an account started years ago at the Wells Fargo in midtown Pearl Handle, for the purpose of digitizing those irreplaceable cultural artifacts. I want the Arts Program, represented by you as Seat, to embrace this effort."

Aaron kept one foot in front of the other as Moses continued.

"We'll officially start once this semester's classes are over and before the Summer Passage begins. The funds will be in their own account, which Pettibone stipulated that only the Seat of the Arts Program can oversee. First thing is, you'll take possession of these funds on behalf of the Arts Program, so that a new account can be opened at Parami's Conscious Credit Union."

"You want *me* to take possession?"

"You'll need to be very discreet concerning all of this. You know how it is with institutions, especially one as small as Parami. Word gets out we've earmarked these funds for Arts, every department and program is going to push for them to be equally dispersed. This restoration project was Willard Pettibone's utmost wish, and I want to see that wish carried out the way he intended."

"What's the time frame?"

"The funds should be secured immediately. You'll be interacting with Wells Fargo's branch president directly. Do you know Madlenka in Commerce and Prosperity?"

"She called me once. I don't think I've ever met her."

"You'll present her with the withdrawn funds, then she'll see to it the transition goes smooth as butter. By July first, when the new fiscal year kicks in, I want you to have devised budget allocations for the Parami Arts Repository, what should be a multiyear project."

Aaron was stunned. Because of the discovery of these long-neglected funds, he wasn't being terminated or even reprimanded, but was included in Moses's long-term plans for Parami, however confounding those plans seemed to be.

AARON BORROWED ONE of Parami's cars, an '80s BMW, for the two things he needed to do that day. First, he drove to Wells Fargo and picked up the cashier's check made out to the Parami Arts Repository, then drove over to one of the university's downtown offices. As Moses had instructed, he walked to Madlenka's cubicle and handed her the check; she beamed and said: "This goes straight to the new account that has been set up."

"Do I get a receipt or anything?"

"Why a receipt? It is Parami money and will now be in Parami's financial institution. You got a withdrawal receipt from Fargo, did you not?"

"After it's deposited in Conscious Credit, please make sure I get a copy."

With that, Aaron set out for Denver International Airport.

Even though Aaron had only seen snaps of him on the internet, Rahsaan Jerome Cooke wasn't difficult to spot. Besides being the only Black man in sight, Rahsaan wore a rust-shaded caftan with several strands of multicolored beads dangling from his neck. Bearded and short, no more than five-seven, he wore a felt hat perched on his head like a bowl that had been upended, and suede desert boots. A weathered leather satchel hung from his shoulder, dangling to his knee.

"Rahsaan Cooke?" Aaron said.

"That is I. And you must be the voice on the phone."

Aaron, introducing himself, assured Rahsaan that it was. "Did you check any luggage?"

"I learned a long time ago to travel light."

They walked to short-term parking, then shared a somewhat solemn ride to Pearl Handle. When they got to town, Rahsaan said, "Mind if we swing by campus on the way to the hotel? I wanna check something while it's still light out."

A warm Friday afternoon. As they passed Parami, it was between classes, and students were strolling on the sidewalks or lounging on the grass.

"Where are all the brothers and sisters?" Rahsaan asked.

Slightly taken aback, Aaron didn't say anything.

"From the look of your website, you'd think Parami was Howard or Fisk or TSU. You must bus in some of those alleged students for picture day."

Aaron laughed, still not knowing what to say.

Rahsaan looked at him. "You're the man who hired me, right?

"Uh-huh."

"Catch much flack for it?"

"A bit."

Rahsaan let out a sigh. "A writer scribbles something one day and people assume that's how you feel *every* day, for the rest of your life. You ever have a headache, a bellyache, just a simple shitty mood? The haters who call me a hater, want to shut me down, have never read anything I've written. They've only read *about* it. Get me to the hotel now, the poet needs a nap."

CHAPTER 34

Who Loves Gangs?

When he arrived that evening at the Plateau Performance Space, Aaron was relieved that there were no protestors in evidence. The cavernous room was packed.

As he read, Rahsaan clutched the podium from both sides, rocking like he was steering a boat through choppy seas. He leaned into the microphone, emitting just the right amount of air, generating just the right volume, with the perfect degree of emphasis, a skilled musician playing a score. Well before the time Rahsaan shifted into what appeared to be his closing piece, Aaron knew he was watching a pro.

Who loves gangs?
I love gangs.
Especially when they're petrifying the white folk
And not banging each other over some meaningless turf war.
Yes, that's right,
Scaring the white establishment shit-silly
Because we're not supposed to be organized and unified,
Are supposed to be loose
And unreliable because it's in their best interest to portray us that way.

Who loves gangs?
I love gangs.

Because it sends the white female contingent
Who secretly like to see us with low-hanging beltlines
And glistening torsos,
That glint in their shifty eyes, knowing they're looking at
Better rappers, better ballers, better every-things.
Who loves gangs?

Scattered voices joined him with "I love gangs." Rahsaan was sent back palpably as though he'd just plugged some device into a socket and received an unanticipated jolt.

Because it scares the academies and universities
Who have always kept us out, yet presume to study us
With their smug and profusely funded sterile probings.
Who loves gangs?

"I love gangs." This time the cry was assumed by half the audience. Rahsaan gave a bemused shrug as he pressed on.

Because it scares the feds when we make drug money for ourselves
And not the domestic military and their Latin-speaking partners.
Who loves gangs?

"I love gangs!" Now the room was booming.

Because we scare the shit out of the Korean grocers
Who jack up the prices and bring their families over to sleep in the store
And work round the clock because you need a green card to work
But not to own,
And when they've gouged the community enough,
They buy another store for the newcomer,
And open their arms to fresh and increasingly exploitative relatives.

Who loves gangs—

"I love gangs!"

Because we in fact outnumber the local police
And can marshal as much firepower and they know it and fear it.
Who loves gangs?

"I love gangs!"

'Cause I know what a crew can do when it's fused as one heart and mind
Just look at Fidel and Che when they were holed up and holy
In the Sierra Maestras.
Who loves gangs?

"I love gangs!!"

Because they make the pollsters and pundits
Clutch their briefcases a little tighter
As they scurry into their glass towers to spread their grimy sound bites
And smarmy scenarios.
Who loves gangs?

"I love gangs!!"

Because they're tapped in and fully equipped and if they chose to,
Could GPS their way to the suburbs
And surround the houses of targeted corporate oppressors.
Who loves gangs?

"I love gangs!!"

'Cause it makes it easier to smash windows
And lift the big-screens and iPods and iPads and iPhones
And jacked-up running shoes designed by buttoned-up yuppies
In the Silicon Valley and Pacific Northwest

Who couldn't produce them unless supported
By so-called Third World sweatshop labor.
Who loves gangs?

"I love gangs!!!"

Who loves gangs?

"I love gangs!!!"

Who loves gangs?

"I love gangs!!!"

Aaron's eyes swept the room. The crowd, almost entirely white, was on its feet, faces flushed and hands clapping.

Rahsaan, still at the podium, was fussing with his sheaf of papers, looking bewildered. He strode off the stage to delirious applause and, as he swept by, Aaron heard him say, "Get me the fuck out of here."

THE QUEEN OF the Rockies Hotel was an aged but recently renovated establishment on the edge of downtown Pearl Handle. Since Rahsaan was staying there and they had a decent bar, Aaron determined it to be the most logical place to have a drink with him. They took a table in the corner and, with no one resembling a waitperson in proximity, Aaron said, "I'll get the drinks. What would you like?"

During the drive to the hotel, Rahsaan had donned a narrow-brimmed charcoal hat with a maroon silk band. "Just a beer. Long as it's not choco-late or oatmeal or raspberry, like some jumped-up milkshake."

Aaron ambled to the bar where the frat-boy bartender was engrossed in his cell phone. Aaron's eyes scanned the row of taps. Mostly micro-brews: a stout, a porter, an IPA—which he ordered for himself—and a Coors Light, which he ordered for Rahsaan.

When Aaron brought the drinks to the table, Rahsaan's attention was on a spring training ballgame being beamed from a high screen in the corner.

Taking the pint glass from Aaron, Rahsaan took a few vigorous gulps. A waitress appeared, a tall blond, most likely an SWU student who, like the barkeep, considered herself meant for much better things than filling orders at the Queen of the Rockies.

"I see you gentlemen got your first round already. Did you pay, or are we on a tab?"

"I paid," said Aaron. Seeing that Rahsaan's glass would soon be empty, he said, "And we'll have two more. I'll have what he's having."

"Coors Light, looks like," said the waitress. She turned and left.

Aaron half expected Rahsaan to make a remark about the beer he was drinking, Coors being notoriously on the right end of the political scale. But Rahsaan's eyes were on the ballgame, where a pair of infielders had trapped a hapless base runner and were wearing him down. When they mercifully tagged him out, Rahsaan turned back to the table. "I love baseball. Probably could have played at least semipro, but other things imposed themselves. Like it says in the Koran: 'If God intends something for you, there's nothing you can do to stop it. If God doesn't want something for you, there's nothing you can do to get it.'" He shrugged. "Something like that, anyway."

The young woman returned with the drinks. "The main reason I took you up on your offer to come here," Rahsaan said, "was because of detective poetics."

"What does that mean?"

"I look at things behind the smokescreen and try to determine what's fueling them." Leaning closer, he lowered his voice. "I noticed something interesting this evening," the poet continued. "Nobody spoke to you. You're all on your own here, aren't you?

"Well. I haven't been here very long."

"Who brought you in?"

"The former . . . president."

"So, that individual jumped ship?"

Aaron nodded his head yes.

"There are clearly two sides at work, the clueless Paramis, who cheered on the reading, thinking I was talking about all those *other* white people, and the cunning, covert fundamentalists, lurking in the shadows. Since you're clearly not in either of those columns, why don't you ask whoever brought you here why they put you between a rock and a hard place?" Rahsaan drew the pint to his lips, taking a gulp this time. "Something's rotten in Dharma, my friend."

CHAPTER 35

Breaking and Entering

Nolan Pickering was homeless because he stopped going home. That is, he stopped spending any time in the shabby, overpriced apartment whose rent his mother had paid in advance for the rest of the school year. The majority of his time was spent outdoors, any possessions he deemed essential stuffed in his backpack. Among these was a yoga mat he slept on, sometimes in the park adjacent to downtown, but more often, and with less likelihood of being roused by the cops, by the river that ran through Pearl Handle.

Nolan couldn't claim to be making new friends, as his vow of silence severely limited his interactions. But most of the town's homeless people knew each other, or knew about each other, and were, for the most part, genial and tolerant, considering Nolan to be some poor, mute runaway kid who somehow ended up on the streets. This was fine with Nolan, as he considered himself a silent bodhisattva who looked upon his fellow sentient beings with wordless, loving compassion. No one suspected that he had a bank account he would dip into with increasing frequency.

Like so many of Pearl Handle's homeless people, Nolan sustained himself by probing the dumpsters behind the restaurants and grocery stores and coffee shops and bars, as well as trash cans, particularly in the pristine, residential neighborhoods. Still in possession of his Parami bus pass, he rode the buses daily. He also made regular visits to Indica at the Can-Abyss Cottage to purchase loaded gummy bears and lollipops. He spent hours at the public library navigating Lawrence Timmons's website, picking up morsels of wisdom to sustain him through the days and nights.

One afternoon Nolan was coming out of the public library and a couple named Claude and Minnie called him over to the bench where they were sorting through their chaotic array of possessions.

"Listen, Quiet Boy," Claude began, using the street name ascribed to Nolan. "Just a friendly heads-up. There's talk floating that you're not a runaway but a trustafarian who dropped out of that high-priced hippie school over on Many Whips Avenue."

"We don't care either way who you really are," said Minnie. "Just felt it fair to warn you."

Nolan looked at them, smiling.

"Thing is," said Claude, "if you're really some rich kid and you really *can* talk—and it don't matter to us if you can or can't—some other folks don't like to be put on, and they might be lookin' to spring somethin' on you."

"And we," added Minnie, "feel you ought to be prepared."

Claude stepped closer, lowering his tone. "If you're gonna be out here, it might be wise for you to have something that will keep anybody from messin' with you. Lucky for you we come across a little equalizer somebody dropped alongside the river. Completely clean, we scraped off the serial number. And if it's true you got money stashed somewhere and can get your hands on it, meet us over at the band shell one hour after dark and we'll fix you up with the means to even things out, should anybody give you any grief."

NOLAN WAS LYING on his back, the night wrapped round him, attuned to the sound of the river. With half-closed eyes, his thoughts lifted, lingered, then floated skyward.

He felt mixed about having a gun in his backpack. Timmons made frequent references to "the warrior spirit." *War* was contained in *warrior*, and weapons were certainly a facet of war. Timmons also wrote: "The enlightened being must be prepared." Well, even the pristine streets of Pearl Handle could turn dangerous, and a gun surely made him more ready for what he might encounter.

It also induced lingering thoughts about his mother. Her trial date kept getting pushed back and was now set for late May, her lawyer saying it would be best for her if Nolan would be there as much as possible. But he hadn't spoken to his mother in a while and now had to admit he was considering—

Thud!

A jolt to his ribs.

"Get up, rich kid."

Nolan scrambled to his feet. Three, no four of them surrounding him in the shadows.

"Got any goodies in that backpack, rich kid?"

"Any crank or cash?"

"Cat got your tongue?"

"How about we take that sash from your stupid bathrobe and wrap it round your neck?"

Nolan felt a tremendous blow to his left cheek, and he went down onto his side. A boot slammed into his right ribcage.

Nolan's mind reeled. These beings, whoever they were, had no glimmer of compassion; if he didn't do something, now, this instant, he could be seriously hurt, even lose his life.

He crawled to his backpack which he'd set beside the yoga mat. Pulling it up to his chest he said, "Is this what you want?"

He felt blood oozing out of his mouth and down his chin.

"Oh, he *can* talk," one of them said, followed by harsh laughter.

Knowing in which pouch he'd tucked the pistol, Nolan shoved his hand in and came up with it.

"What the hell's he got?" one of them said.

Nolan's finger found the trigger. He pointed the barrel skyward and the gun kicked.

His ears rang as he sat motionless. He was alone, the four having fled in what seemed like every direction. The .38 felt heavy and hot. Looking around, he determined that his attackers were gone.

Nolan rolled up the yoga mat and shoved it in his backpack. He needed to get away from there, go someplace else. A sharp, acrid smell in the air, the same as that terrible night in that dark and doomed mansion in Virginia.

NOLAN SPENT THE following day as usual, riding the bus and sitting at one of the library computers. He considered going to the hospital, as the left side of his face was swollen and that ringing remained in his head, but he didn't feel like filling out forms and answering questions that would likely lead to conversations with the cops. Timmons had cautioned in one of his lectures: "Stay low and avoid litigation."

As it grew dark then late, and he'd raided the bins of the Tuscan Kitchen and Bangkok Palace, Nolan found himself walking by Parami's Timmons House, headquarters of the Arts Program. A set of small windows lined the foundation, indication that the one-story structure had a basement.

Nolan went over, crouched, and peered in the nearest basement window, whose frame looked big enough to slip through. He pulled out the .38 and, with the butt of it, shattered the glass.

AARON WAS IN his office, working late. As the Spring Passage deepened and midterms approached, he'd taken to coming in after hours. Without the hum of daytime activity, he was able to get much more done. Besides that, he kept a bottle of Tito's at the ready and found it enjoyable to savor it as he sifted through his tasks. The only drawback was that he found Timmons House spooky at night. That's why, at the sound of breaking glass, he froze.

Sounds from the basement. Aaron had never been down there; nobody had, as far as he knew, for years. A door led down from the first-floor bathroom but was largely inaccessible, with mops and brooms and industrial-sized plastic buckets of cleaning supplies stacked in front of it.

More creaking and rustling. Aaron thought of calling the number for campus security, even though, once the campus shut down, he'd never glimpsed a security guard. *What about calling 911?*

If it were some animal—a raccoon or a possum, or God forbid a skunk—how would he feel about bringing the police out for that?

He rose from his desk, stepped out of his office, and crossed the reception area.

Maybe it was, Aaron told himself, an actual security guard. But how did they get down there? Aaron heard something, someone, ascending the stairs. The doorknob turned, then an attempt was made to force open the door. Aaron found the light switch, and the tight, cluttered space was filled with glaring brightness. The door lurched, and a broom, a mop, and a couple of buckets collapsed to the floor. Whoever was on the other side of the door put their shoulder to it, and more cleaning supplies were jostled enough for a widening crack to appear. Aaron stood watching as the door opened and, inch by inch, the scarlet-clad form revealed itself.

"My God, Nolan. What the hell are you doing?"

Although unnerved, Aaron acted as though a former student breaking into Timmons House in the middle of the night was a completely normal occurrence. "Come on in."

Leading the way back to his office, he added, "Just out of curiosity, what are you doing, busting in here?"

"Nowhere else to go," said Nolan.

Still feigning normalcy, and resigning himself to the fumes from the infernal bathrobe, Aaron sat behind his desk and motioned toward the only other chair in the room.

Nolan's eyes alighted on the bottle of Tito's in front of Aaron. "Could I have some of that?"

Aaron fetched a compostable cup that the university regularly supplied and poured some vodka. "Sorry, I don't have any ice."

"This is great," said Nolan, as he threw back the contents of the cup, effectively downing a double.

"That was quick. You drink a lot?" asked Aaron.

"Hardly ever. Can I have another?"

"Just one. Then I suggest you slow down. I don't want to have to carry you out of here. What happened to your face?"

Nolan sat, then talked about living on the streets, sleeping by the river, getting jumped in the middle of the night. "But I scared them off, I'm proud to say."

"You fought back?"

"No, this." Nolan pulled the .38 from his bathrobe pocket.

Aaron pushed his chair back and stood up. "Whoa, what are you doing? Put that away."

Nolan looked at the gun as if it had just sprouted in his palm, then set it on the desk. "Are you gonna call the police, Mr. Motherway?"

Aaron glanced at the gun as though it were a grenade whose pin had been yanked. "Do you think I need to, Nolan?"

The kid shook his head. "I wish you wouldn't." He cradled his arms and lay his head on the desk. "I'm just so tired, Mr. Motherway. So goddamn tired."

Aaron took a moment, then said, "At least you're talking."

Nolan raised his head. "My mother is accused of killing my father. She's going to stand trial for his murder."

Aaron looked back at him and felt himself fill up with something he couldn't name. "I know, Nolan. I know all about that."

"How? How do you know?"

"I was told before you got here. I'm not surprised you dropped out. That's a lot for anybody to handle."

The young man stared at Aaron. "I don't know what to do, Mr. Motherway."

"I don't think you should be walking around with a gun."

"That gun saved my life."

"If you got stopped by the cops it could go badly for you. It's not registered, I'll bet. You don't have a permit."

Nolan shook his head. "I don't want to get rid of it. It saved me."

Aaron took a moment. "Tell you what. Why don't you leave it here? I'll keep it for you, and nobody will know I have it. Then once you're, you know, feeling better, get in touch and I'll give it back to you."

"You promise?"

"I swear."

"You promise to keep it right here in that desk? I don't want you stashing it someplace where somebody might come across it and take it or turn it in."

"I'm not gonna touch it, Nolan. Firearms aren't something I have any experience with."

Nolan handed the gun to Aaron, who slipped it into the top drawer, underneath a stack of papers. After a deep breath, Nolan said, "I can't live on the streets anymore, I don't feel safe. Can't go back to school, I'd just drop out again. Tell me what to do, Mr. Motherway."

Aaron took a deep breath of his own. "What happened to your father was terrible. What's happening with your mother is terrible."

"What do I do?" the boy asked softly.

"You need to go home, Nolan."

A moment. "You mean back to my apartment?"

Aaron shook his head. "No, I mean home."

CHAPTER 36

Liturgy in Literature

High Importance! From Betsy Cohn, Director of ID (Inclusion &
Diversity): Authentic Senegalese Dance has been canceled after
the three women enrolled withdrew in protest of being required
to wear skirts during class sessions. While Bamba Seck (male
adjunct instructor who is from Senegal) claims that skirts are
in keeping with traditional Senegalese garb for all genders, the
departing women feel that even if the other five students (who
identify as male) choose to wear skirts, for women, it still represents role oppression and should not be dictated by anyone,
especially a male teaching Senegalese Dance anywhere besides
Senegal.

Viti appeared in the doorway of Aaron's office. "There's a student
wanting to see you. September Riley."

"Send her in."

Viti stepped closer, lowering her voice. "Some kind of crisis. She
went to Student Success, but Missy Samuels was having lunch at her
desk and told her to come back at the end of the day."

September was a tall young woman, large-boned, wearing a burgundy Parami hoodie, jeans strategically ripped, pink Converse tennis shoes, an olive-green backpack strapped to her shoulders. Clearly agitated, face flushed, at a loss of what to do with her hands.

Aaron gestured for her to take a seat, but September remained on her feet, pacing.

"This isn't what I signed up for," said September. "This is *not* what I signed up for."

Aaron watched as she paced back and forth.

"I don't care what they say, there's no way I'm going to burn for all eternity."

"What who says?"

September stopped moving, took a step back. "You're not one of them, even though you put me in that class." Her eyes narrowed. "Or maybe you are and you're just not acting like it."

"September, sit down, please."

She plopped into the chair, then plunged her face into her large hands. She looked up at Aaron, eyes poking through splayed fingers. "I'm not going to burn, not for all eternity. If God's good like she says he is, then why would he incinerate one of his children? Doesn't that sound more like something Satan would do?" She shook her head, then her whole body convulsed as though she'd been doused with cold water. "Her voice gets into my head. I've hardly slept since last week's class. How can I get her out of my head?"

"Who?"

Now September appeared limp, legs extended in front of her, shoulders sagging. "Frances Thrush. Her whole class of Troops. They want to cleanse me, but I won't let them."

"Cleanse you?"

"They convinced me to surrender myself over to the Lord and Master the third week of class, but today I took it back. It's not what she should be doing in a writing class. Have you seen her syllabus?" Both hands plunged into her backpack and came up with some crumpled, stapled sheets, which she shoved at Aaron. "I came here to study writing and literature. This is not what I signed up for."

AARON STOOD IN the hallway, waiting for Frances Thrush to wind up her class. A minute before 5:50 p.m., when class was to conclude, a set of voices were reciting words he could not decipher. He stepped closer, stopped short of pressing his ear to the door, but still couldn't determine what they were saying.

The door finally swung open, and he waited until the last student filed out. When Aaron entered the classroom, Frances Thrush stood at her desk, stuffing a set of papers into a manila envelope. Aaron was freshly aware that he had yet to exchange a word with her, nor had he ever seen her up close. She had short brown hair, subtly frosted, and wore a lime-green pantsuit. Her face was unremarkable except that her nose, of the button variety, took a sharp bend to the right. "Hello there," she said, clearly surprised.

"I don't believe we've met. I'm Aaron Motherway, Seat of the Arts Program."

Frances pointedly ignored him as she shoved the envelope into a leather shoulder bag, open on the desk.

"And how was class today?" Aaron read from the syllabus he was holding. "Images of the Cross in the Poetics of Emily Dickinson . . . Nathaniel Hawthorne and the Sixth Commandment . . . Moby Dick as It Relates to the Loaves and the Fishes."

Frances's lips were trembling. "Where did you—"

"Where did I get it? It came from a student who's paying a lot of money for what's supposed to be a traditional lit seminar."

"None of the other students are complaining."

"So, all on your own, you decided to come to Parami and teach"—he glanced again at the syllabus—"Liturgy in Literature, not at all what you were contracted to do."

"You have no idea. Students love this class. It's changing their lives."

"Not the student who just left my office, and who's probably leaving the university."

"September Riley, a lost soul. She had embraced the course but her own selfishness and devilish thinking made her lose her way."

"We're not dispensing doctrine here, Ms. Thrush."

"You can't tell me what to teach and what not to teach. Next year I'll be in charge, and you'll be on the street where you belong."

Aaron was both furious and fascinated. No matter what Moses said about putting him in charge of the Parami Arts Repository, here was Aaron, face to face with the one chosen to replace him.

CHAPTER 37

Mercy

The first day of spring break, Aaron drove to DIA, got his ticket and boarding pass from the kiosk, went through the post-9/11 humiliations of security, then boarded the silver tube for a nonstop flight to Fort Lauderdale.

He rented a metallic-blue Honda Civic, drove south on perilous I-95, and checked in to a cozy motel on the beach.

Waking just after dawn, he asked for directions at the desk, then strolled along the ocean, three-quarters of a mile, to the Mercy Café.

He was expecting a bleached-out wooden shack with surfboards parked on the side, the kind of ramshackle establishment you might come across in one of the beach towns south of LA. But like everything else in Highland Beach, Florida, the Mercy Café was gleaming and bright.

Aaron took a table in the corner, ordered two fried eggs sunny-side up with a side of cottage cheese, sourdough toast, and coffee.

He took time with breakfast, reading the *Sun Sentinel* when, through the glass revolving door, looking very much like he appeared in his Christmas letter, Terence Dillard breezed in.

Dillard greeted the fifty-something waitress and was seated at a table for two. Aaron turned the newspaper back to page one—this time reading a few articles he skimmed over before—ordered a cinnamon roll for dessert, and downed two and a half more cups of coffee.

When Dillard called for the check, Aaron went over and pulled out the chair across from him. Dillard appeared startled but rallied with a smile, half rising before lowering his tanned, lanky body back into his chair.

"Aaron Motherway, what on earth are you doing in Highland Beach?"

Aaron smiled. "I came to see you, Doctor Dillard."

WALKING ON THE sand, Aaron and Dillard had the silver-blue glare of the Atlantic surging beside them. Aaron stooped and picked up a couple of shells. He inspected one, put in in his pocket, then tossed the other aside.

"When I saw the video, the one of the speech you made for last year's Synod, I asked myself, 'why would someone who clearly had big plans for the institution he was running abruptly announce his retirement?' What are you, sixty-two, sixty-three? Only two years earlier you'd achieved the level of university president. Why would you retire unless somebody made it really worth your while to do so?"

Dillard's sunny demeanor of minutes before had darkened into someone from the witness protection program who found himself in the company of one of the sinister figures from his past.

"Coming from a traditional academic background, I just couldn't make the not-for-profit model work. All the old-line Paramis come off like they're open and amendable but, as I'm sure you're finding out, are quite intractable."

Aaron stopped walking. Dillard halted and turned to him as though on a leash.

"Why me?" Aaron asked. "You must have known by the summer you were going to leave."

Dillard drew in the kind of breath a man facing a firing squad might take, savoring his last drag on a cigarette. The waves, the breeze, then: "Sandy Sue Lundvall," Dillard said in a tone that seemed like sand had somehow seeped into his mouth.

"What?"

"You can't tell me you don't remember her."

Aaron's mind was reeling. "Sandy Sue Lundvall, the editor of *Absinthe?*" A short-lived literary journal when Aaron was at Michigan State.

Dillard was walking again, staring ahead as though trying to put distance between himself and Aaron. "You had a little fling with her the month before graduation. I'm sure it didn't mean anything to you, but it did to her—and it surely did to me." In an even more embittered tone he said, "Sandy Sue was the love of my life."

Dillard halted once more, then spoke like one recalling a narrative he knew by heart. "I never liked you, Aaron. Even before you screwed the woman I wanted to spend the second half of my life with. You were cynical, sarcastic, and from what I could tell, totally without a moral compass.

"Bringing you in may have seemed like an opportunity, but I knew those looneys in the Arts Program were never going to accept you, knew you'd get caught up in something that couldn't succeed and that you were in no way prepared for. Yes, I knew I was leaving at that point, I'd made my devil's bargain. I set you up, knowing it wouldn't last." A harsh laugh. "So, you figured some of it out, and that's why you're here asking questions. I signed a nondisclosure, and I'm not putting that at risk, especially not for someone I've loathed as long as I have you."

Dillard turned, then continued down the beach, leaving Aaron standing in the salt-tinged air.

PART THREE
LEAVING

CHAPTER 38

Walking Wisdom

Chodak awoke in the mountains outside San Francisco. He stood and faced the sun. He bobbed his head back and forth, rotated his right shoulder forward, then his left. Reversing the direction of his left, he then rotated his right shoulder backward. After that, both shoulders at once; forward, backward. His physical form, fluid and resilient for four decades, was exhibiting traces of stiffness and wear. He decided not to include his leg dips and stretches, even though today he'd do a great deal of walking.

Having landed the previous afternoon at San Francisco International Airport, Chodak was heading east. His mother lived nearby, but he had not seen her in decades, and renewing their relationship was not the purpose of his arrival in the U.S.

He planned not to solicit rides, but if anyone were to stop for him, he would gladly take up their offer. Yesterday, setting out from the teeming airport, Chodak had been fortunate that a car with a kind American fellow at the wheel had driven him well outside the urban mass.

Chodak would continue traveling as far as possible until he reached his destination, approximately twelve hundred miles away.

This was the first time he'd been in America in thirty years. His mother, Dahna, brought him here when he was seven, three years after the High Lama dropped his physical form, and a mound of garments were piled at the end of the dusty central street.

That long-ago day, Chodak did not want to go outside, wanted to stay curled up in his narrow but comfortable bed. His mother, as though holding some secret, made him get up and join the other children, some from distant villages.

Chodak had felt strange at that time, chest heavy and limbs, particularly his arms, weighted. He recalled having the thought that if anyone were to fling his small body into the river, he would surely sink. His tongue felt thick and his throat dry. Not a wholly unpleasant feeling, but it did feel foreign, like his skin and bones were wrapped around some new and different inner body.

That day, once Chodak was outside, he noticed the pale, sinewy, long-haired man whose name, he would later learn, was Lawrence Timmons. They locked eyes, and Chodak somehow saw into him. Timmons struck him as a kind and gentle soul, although the man's eyes held not answers, but questions. Parts of his aura appeared weak and underdeveloped.

Chodak took his place among the children and, after episodes of chanting followed by periods of silence, Tinley, one of the High Lama's devotees, announced it was time; the child who recognized the High Lama's sole garment in the massive pile should come forward and claim it.

A few tried to move, but it seemed some unseen force was holding them in place. Chodak was immobile but, like a breath had come over him from without and then within, felt weightless as he approached the mound of garments, flinging several aside before taking hold of a peach-shaded sari he wrapped around his tiny frame.

The elders bowed, then knelt, and the children followed. The American Timmons awkwardly did the same, everyone present knowing that the High Lama's essence was now attached to Chodak.

Dahna wept, for even when carrying Chodak in her womb, she knew this child was meant for vast, world-changing things.

For the first few years Chodak was dutiful, studying the teachings of the High Lama, acquainting—most thought reacquainting—himself with embedded wisdom. Dahna kept in touch with Lawrence Timmons, who had returned to the U.S. and was gathering a following based largely upon teachings he'd been exposed to in Tibet. Timmons agreed with Dahna that Chodak coming to North America and delivering a series of lectures would be inspiring for all who heard them, the start of the enlightened child's global life.

Timmons, on the lecture circuit himself, arranged with his speaker's bureau to take on Chodak as a client. A major promotion firm was enlisted to lay the groundwork for a three-month tour, west coast to east.

The initial engagements were in Seattle, San Francisco, and Los Angeles, major centers with significant percentages of their populations, since the 1960s, dipping into Eastern thought and teachings. Chodak, unlike the robed and white-haired gurus blazing those trails at that moment, was considered to hold timeless wisdom far beyond his sentient chronology.

What his mother, what Timmons and his promoters and nobody else counted on, was that such lack of current experience might render the child vulnerable to worldly temptations. In San Francisco, Berkeley to be precise, on the third night of his tour, Chodak tasted for the first time the wonders of Baskin-Robbins ice cream.

Initially, this was thought to be cute, and the newsletter generated to promote the tour played up the tiny guru's fondness for the frozen dessert. By Chicago, Baskin-Robbins was no longer a treat but a staple, Chodak sampling every one of the brand's thirty-one flavors, consuming upwards of a dozen pints a day. On the final leg of the tour, Boston's Symphony Hall, backstage selections of Baskin-Robbins were, for the first time since their introduction, not on site.

Chodak, exhausted from ninety days on the road, threw a rock-star fit, demanding that one of his attendees go out and procure the frozen treat, or he would refuse to take the stage. A driver was dispatched, then gone quite a while. When he returned with Breyers and not Chodak's brand of choice, the boy petulantly sampled one spoonful before declaring he must have Baskin-Robbins and nothing else. By the time four pints were secured and delivered, three-fourths of the audience had departed.

A feature writer from the *Globe* was lurking backstage, and the following day, the headline Tiny Guru's Tantric Tantrum was picked up by the wire services. Chodak's tour turned into a national punchline. Widow Dahna, who'd met a moneyed, Palo Alto–based divorcé during the opening dates of the tour, refused to return home with Chodak, sending her now corpulent son back in the company of Tinsley, a disillusioned disciple.

Everything shifted: Dahna settling in the Silicon Valley and starting a second family; Chodak returning to his village and quietly completing his education without much distinction. He eventually landed in Singapore, working as a noodle chef in a series of eating establishments of varying quality. Chodak became neither a householder nor a monk and never spoke of his past. On occasion, he felt glints of . . . intuition, precognition . . . some sense that the power once guiding him had not been completely extinguished.

He took up meditation again, and the image of Lawrence Timmons, whom he'd not spoken to for years, would regularly manifest. He knew that an American school had been founded around Timmons. Chodak had never been there, only knew its name and that it was located near the Rocky Mountains, but when it arose in meditation, the images were alarming and horrific.

STAMFORD'S WIFE, DELSEY, had gone to celebrate Easter in Chicago with her sister, so he was on his own. He seized the opportunity to arrange for Madlenka to meet him at 11:00 p.m. at Humphey's, a restaurant and bar on the edge of Pearl Handle that stayed open until midnight.

Madlenka arrived, looking as though she'd put some thought into what she was wearing, a velvet-collared jacket over a tight sweater. If she had any notion that this meeting would mean the resumption of their affair, the reverend was all business.

"We have a problem," he said, once she settled across from him in an oversized booth.

"What problem is this?"

Stamford leaned forward, lowering the volume of his already low voice. "Aaron Motherway."

"I know. He keeps asking for a receipt from the deposit at Conscious Credit. I told him it is unnecessary; the account is all set up."

She pulled out a Spirit, but when Stamford glared at her, she just held it and didn't dip into her bag for her lighter.

"I received an email he sent out," Stamford said, "informing the university that he's firing one of the faith-based instructors I brought in, Frances Thrush. He quoted the still-unrevised *Preceptor Compendium*, and sure enough, it says a program Seat can terminate a preceptor if the Seat is the preceptor's immediate supervisor." Stamford's eyes swept the room, then lighted once more on Madlenka. "It must be dawning on him what's happening at Parami. He must have also figured out that my putting him in charge of the Arts Repository doesn't mean his contract is going to be renewed. I need to activate the things I've been saving up to use against him."

"And you think those will weigh enough?"

"I'm already marshaling as much opposition to him as I can with staff and preceptors, both old and new. Students, too. It shouldn't be hard. A lot of the faith-based Troops are up in arms over the firing of Frances Thrush. Frances herself is outraged and has already stirred a lot of support on the internet." His eyes swept the room again. "When our friend Motherway comes back from break, I'm going to see to it he has his hands full."

Madlenka, her voice at its own measured volume, said, "What am I to do about him asking for the deposit receipt?"

"As we know too well, you have a direct line into all the accounts at Conscious Credit. Have you replenished the accounts with the Arts Repository monies?"

Madlenka smiled. "All healthy once more. Ten thousand here, twenty thousand there. They got used to Parami making emergency withdrawals and deposits, moving dollars around. And since Conscious Credit knows not where such funds originated, no one is ever to know."

Stamford smiled. "I had somebody look into our friend Motherway's finances. Seems he's being sued by his former insurance company for massive, unpaid medical bills. So, when all this comes down, it will appear that Motherway's contract wasn't going to be renewed, and out of desperation, he tried to claim for himself these seemingly forgotten funds he came across. We'll accuse him of stashing them somewhere, and he'll of course, deny it."

"So, I am never to give him a receipt?"

"He was issued a Parami computer, and I have access to all the preceptors' passwords. I'll go into his office after hours and create a receipt that I'll give to you. Make sure you hand it to him yourself, so it doesn't go through campus mail or, God forbid, email. He's appointed his Protocol Facilitator to take over Frances Thrush's classes, so I'll let you know when she will be in class and not in the office, so it will just be you and him. When the time comes, all you'll need to do is say he's lying, you never gave it to him. Your word against his. Motherway will be left holding a phony receipt we can prove was generated by his Parami computer."

CHAPTER 39

Blowback

Aaron's appreciation of the seasons dated back to his childhood and went in natural order. He liked spring the best, whose warmth and verdant quality would be intoxicating after a long, gloomy, Michigan winter. Summers were hot and green, the long days stretching into nights, so different from the gelid darkness of months and even weeks before. Fall days could be lovely, and many Michiganders claimed them as their favorite time; radiant, glistening leaves and football stadiums brimming with cheering fans. But Aaron always felt melancholy from September to November, knowing that winter would soon descend with its treacherous icy roads and black dawns.

In LA he'd escaped all that—the changes, the barometric extremes—the thermostat leveled at seventy-two, interrupted only by periodic rain.

But here he was, back in climate, not having realized how heavy the winter had been on him. This, the first day of classes after spring break, he felt buoyant and fresh, light of foot and frame, as though he'd greeted the morning by flinging off a heavy coat.

He'd decided to walk to Parami and left plenty of time for that purpose.

Approaching the campus, Aaron saw that the driveway between

Timmons House and a string of classroom structures was lined on either side with what appeared to be students, several waving placards. A sign on one side said: Frances, Not Motherway! A sign on the other side: Save the Prairie Dogs!

As Aaron kept moving toward the back entrance to Timmons House, each side of the crowd, thirty or forty in each sector, surged toward him.

"Idiot!" a young woman screamed in his left ear.

"Bastard!" a young man screamed in his right.

The swarm of faces were red and contorted and it occurred to Aaron that physical assault was a possibility. He managed to keep moving toward the door at the rear of Timmons House. As he got closer, neither faction appeared inclined to follow him in, and Aaron gratefully slammed the door behind him.

Viti was standing in front of her desk, with an expression of grave concern. "I would have warned you," she said, "but I only got here a few minutes ago myself."

Aaron looked around as if to locate something to lean against. "What the hell's going on?"

"Frances Thrush's students, the Troops, they call themselves, are up in arms about her being fired."

Trying to regulate his breath, Aaron managed, "There's two groups out there."

"The other is from STOP, Sadistic Treatment of Pollock. They're claiming on their website that the Arts Program—meaning you—have been engaged in rodent genocide, and they're convinced the prairie dogs are next."

Viti took a step closer. "I know you sent out an email announcing that I'll be stepping into Frances Thrush's classes, but it looks like her students are boycotting."

Aaron felt a wave of anger. "Then they're going to fail." He added, somewhat feebly, "Miss two classes and you fail."

"Plus, the Arts Program has received three emails addressed to you and I'm copied on them: Elia Adank, Katryn Burley, and even Connie Yang, saying that having me teach trivializes the program because I'm not a writer."

"Who's Connie Yang?"

"The Long March . . . "

Aaron nodded. "Have you gotten hold of Randall Hendricks's syllabus, the one he's using in class, that is?"

"I double-checked. He's teaching mostly goth material. Poe, H. P. Lovecraft . . . no gospel passages or anything."

Mildly mollified, Aaron said, "Your class is due to start in a few minutes. Please show up for it. Screw what Elia or Katryn or Chairman Mao has to say."

"Okay, but I may be lecturing to just September Riley." She started to go, then said, "There's a guy waiting in your office. I told him to make an appointment, but he was pretty insistent on seeing you."

AARON LISTENED AS Harold Black Kettle addressed him from the other side of the desk.

"My daughter attended school here, a little over two decades ago. Part of her reason for wanting to study writing was that she had grown up hearing from me the stories of the Cheyenne people. I taught her these in Tséhésenéstsestòtse, now spoken only in parts of Montana and Oklahoma, a language that is endangered. She wanted to make those stories into a book. While she was here, a newly arrived professor encouraged her, said he would help her put into English those stories of our people. He arranged a course in which he was the teacher and she was his sole student. Sad to say, there was more going on than just those stories. Although she finished the book, the relationship fell apart and she left her studies before taking her degree. Out of spite, that professor refused to return the book.

"She has a good life now. A husband—not one of our people, but a good man. They raised three children out in Eugene, Oregon. That teacher has no right to be withholding stories that are not his. Mr. Motherway, I want my daughter to publish those stories and need you to help get her book back from Philip Pristley."

Aaron's office door swung open.

"I have brought your receipt," said Madlenka, stepping forward and handing a slip of paper to Aaron. Her head turned as she noted someone else in the room.

"Marie?" said Harold Black Kettle.

"Madlenka," she replied, her demeanor clouding as she took in the unexpected visitor. "You are clearly mixing me up with somebody else."

She left as awkwardly as she had entered.

Getting to his feet, Harold Black Kettle appeared vaguely distressed. "You have my contact information. I'm driving out to Oregon this weekend to see my daughter. If I could have the book before then, I will be eternally grateful." At the door, he turned back. "That woman who was just in here: Is she rich?"

"Rich?" Aaron echoed. "I don't think so. Where do you think you know her from?"

"The Redwing Casino," Harold shook his head, smiling ruefully. "I've never seen anybody lose so much money in such a short time."

■ ■ ■

Opal's upcoming installation, *Red Icons*, will be a collection of religious statues adorned with the artist's own menstrual blood. The collection will be viewed by invitation only. A fee of $7.50 for students and $12.50 for the general public will be collected at the door. Only professional clerics, upon proof of occupation, will be admitted free. In addition, a one-of-a-kind hemp-bound guest book with handwritten comments from attendees will be offered on eBay to the highest bidder.

Axis was sharing a table with Opal in the Enlightened Coffee Shop, the younger woman's infamy and her affair with Philip Priestly having roused Axis's attention. "Congratulations," she said. "Your concept appears to be causing a stir."

"People are trashing it all over the web," said Opal. "But I've already heard from several galleries who want it to travel there. Can't wait to reveal that people are getting all in a wad about a totally made-up event."

"Never underestimate the gullibility of . . . whatever that saying is."

Opal took a sip of her cappuccino, then said, "You ever heard of a dude named Hank Gaffney?"

Axis's lips parted slightly, then she set her coffee cup on its saucer. "You don't know who Hank Gaffney is?"

Opal shrugged. "I've heard of him, of course. Can't say I really know him yet."

"Yet?"

"He's been emailing and texting ever since I started promoting *Red Icons* online, offering advice and such. He somehow caught on that's it's a conceptual event and he seemed to like it even more. He wants me to meet him at the Queen of the Rockies, where he's staying."

Axis freshly studied her young protégé. "Hank Gaffney's in Pearl Handle?"

"Got in this morning and called me. Said he was coming but I didn't take him seriously." Then, "He sounds pretty old. How old is he?"

"I met him through my brother back in London. Must be close to eighty by now. Quite the ladies' man, as they used to say. Don't think he ever married. Came up through the Lower East Side, then made his fortune, bought a lot of beach property in Montauk."

"So, he's rich and . . . *rich?*"

"I can't believe he got in touch with you, and you never even checked his wiki page or anything." Axis continued. "Last I heard, one of his latest sculptures sold at Christie's for over a mil." She shot Opal a look. "Hank Gaffney can open any door; locked, unlocked, hidden. Linked to every board or foundation you can name. If he came all the way to Pearl Handle, you can wager you're the only reason he made the trip. Make sure you go meet him."

Another moment. "What about Philip?"

"You're a smart sort, Opal, so do something smart here." Her tone shifted as though a cloud were sweeping past. "Toss Philip Pristley on the junk heap." Axis's smile returned. "Fancy something else? I'm feeling like a triple-shot vanilla latte."

CHAPTER 40

Holy War in the Rockies

The east side of the main campus, known as Timmons Grove, between Timmons Library and Timmons Administration Center, had been converted into a student campground. The students, however, were in two entirely different camps. One, the Troops, were twenty-four seven protesting the firing of Frances Thrush by Aaron Motherway. The other, from STOP, camped out in solidarity with—but not in proximity to—Parami's population of prairie dogs, whose domain was the front yard of Timmons House, on the far west side of the campus.

The camps were ensconced on either side of the field, one with a set of tents belonging to the Troops, orderly and pristine with an American flag, plus a table with stacks of printed handouts and twenty-dollar T-shirts that read: Free Frances! The other had sleeping bags and yoga mats strewn precariously with a huge banner that said: Prairie Dog Power! The common ground was that both contingents were on strike, encouraging all enrolled students to refrain from attending classes.

This was the scene that Chodak encountered upon arriving at the Parami campus. Dressed in his peach-shaded sari, he carried only a loose silk bag with his scant possessions, including his tightly secured bedroll. Chodak perceived immediately the different qualities of the two encampments: one, stern but stringent, the other, empathetic yet chaotic and disordered. He wondered if the disparity between the two would be the trigger for the devastation that had invaded his consciousness.

So tired he felt a glow emanating from him, he chose a patch of ground between the rival assemblies. In the blazing daylight—legs folded, spine straight, eyes half-open, and palms upturned in supplication—Chodak began his inner chant.

AARON SENT AN email informing Philip Pristley a request had come from a former student that the material she had generated while studying with him be returned. Two hours later, he impulsively called the number listed on the preceptor roster. Pristley answered after several rings.

"Philip, this is Aaron Motherway. Did you get the email I sent?"

"About somebody who studied with me twenty years ago? There was no book of hers, there *is* no book." Pristley's voice sounded hollow. "I'm going through some stuff here, man. Personal stuff."

Aaron had heard from Viti that Opal dumped him for some famous sculptor. Then Philip said, "Come to think of it, I might still have the course notes. I'll leave them in a box, a very *small* box, on the front porch. Since you have my number, I assume you have my address."

PRISTLEY'S HOUSE WAS a ramshackle cottage on a tidy, residential block. There was indeed a front porch but no box containing two-decade-old course notes.

Aaron pressed the ancient bell, buzzer, whatever the hell sound it was supposed to make, but it seemed to have fallen silent. He knocked, then pounded on the front door. No movement from inside, although he did sense rustling from behind one of the curtains.

When Aaron returned to his office empty-handed, he was surprised to find Mitchell Amritt sitting at Viti's desk. "Your Protocol Facilitator wasn't around, so I figured I'd just wait for you."

"Come into my office," Aaron said, and Mitchell followed him in.

"I thought I'd come over and give you fair warning."

Aaron braced himself.

"I was up by the Presider's office and heard Moses telling Kevin he was gonna call the cops because you'd violated some restraining order?"

Bird blew alto. "That's right, I did."

"It's less than two weeks till the end of Spring Passage. Maybe Moses won't get around to calling. Maybe it'll be a low priority and the cops won't rush right over. If you're lucky, you might be able to slip away at the end of the school year."

"Thanks for telling me, Mitchell."

"You're a good dude, Aaron. I appreciate that you didn't tell anybody that getting rid of the mice was a collaborative project."

"My idea, no need to drag you into it."

"Not that I won't be fired anyway, given the biblical wave that's sweeping over this place."

Pristley, course notes, how could I fall for such bullshit?

"After that scene went down with Thaddeus Fogarty, he became a national pariah, but so did I. Parami didn't fire me. Not many institutions would have kept me on. That's why it's such a shame it's all coming to an end."

Aaron could hear the emotion as Mitchell pulled out a near-empty pack of Marlboro Lights. "Look at me, all this stress has made me go back to actual smoking. Mind if I light up?"

Aaron shook his head. "Sorry, Mitchell. They're merely camping out over the mice. If anybody found out I let you smoke in here, we'd be burned at the stake."

LESLIE KROLL LOVED the internet. You could find almost anyone and keep up with details of their life. That's how he discovered that Parami University would be honoring Elia Adank at its commencement and how, once he decided to attend this unholy event, he learned how to make a bomb.

He did so step by crucial step, not the sloppy, impulsive manner that led to him botching Adank's reading at the Banks Gallery. That had been a blessing really, that cheap, plastic lighter failing to ignite. No, this action would be a work of art, would make history, so he approached it with the care in which he maintained his glob.

He purchased ten 50-pound bags of ammonium nitrate, enough to fertilize over an acre of farmland. Renting a storage space, he then packed the explosives in four 55-gallon drums. To this he added one and three-quarters crates of eighteen-inch-long Tovex sausages, twenty pounds of shock tube, and one hundred twenty-five electric blasting caps.

Renting a truck, Leslie nailed boards to hold four barrels in place. He arranged the barrels to form a shaped charge, then tamped the aluminum side panel of the truck with bags of ammonium nitrate to direct the blast in the desired direction, destroying the target and everything within a four-block radius; a blast of twelve hundred and fifty pounds of TNT.

He would have seven minutes to light the fuse and get away.

CHAPTER 41

Commencement

Parami commencement always took place the second Saturday in May, populated not only with graduating students but with preceptors and staff, out-of-town family, and still-enrolled friends, around five hundred in all. The day was bright and clear, and Timmons Grove was pristine, both sets of protesters having left, the non-Troops under Moses's threat of criminal trespass.

The ceremony began with the preceptors being led to the front of the tent by an early Timmons disciple whose *shehnai*, a traditional Indian woodwind, had delighted the school's founder during Parami's early days.

Although Aaron was certain to be fired, he wanted to see his students—especially the ones who'd supported him—receive their diplomas. Having skipped the procession, he took a seat on the aisle.

Flanking Moses on the dais were this year's faith-based student speaker, as well as Garrett Landis, Republican state senator from Jackson Hole. Off to the side was an empty chair, which Aaron assumed was for Elia Adank, retiring preceptor. Aaron wondered if Elia would offer any kind of speech and, if so, in what language.

Moses had not announced that Landis would deliver the commencement address until the end of the semester. Landis, an emerging ultraconservative voice in the state, was especially outspoken on what he termed the lunatic-fringe public schools and state university system. He had not announced his candidacy, but it was generally assumed he would run for governor in 2016. No wonder that Moses had kept Landis's appearance under wraps until the last moment. Having a right-wing legislator speaking at graduation might spark a protest from the graduating and remaining secular students.

Aaron then saw what he had not taken in before.

At the edge of Timmons Grove was a single figure in a peach-shaded robe, arms slightly extended, palms open in supplication. *Parami's last meditator.*

In the glaring sunlight, Moses took the podium.

"May Parami University become what it has always strived to be," said Moses, "a beacon of wisdom and compassion and enlightenment. May its Mindfulness mission be not its own mind, but be guided by the Mind of the One true and everlasting . . . "

Aaron felt himself overcome by emotion. The experiment that had been Parami was over, once a vital and valid alternative, replaced by a sanctimonious, intolerant contingent. Parami's undoing was that they themselves had become in their own way self-absorbed and intolerant. *Why couldn't both exist? Why did they need to annihilate each other?*

Those thoughts lingered for a moment, then he felt himself tip. After a rush of panic, as he'd experienced at the hospital after his accident, he was out of his body, hovering, taking in the scene. Hundreds of people, all listening to Stamford Moses, who Aaron couldn't hear. What he did hear was a low hum as he floated west, the mountains in the distance. He glanced back to see if he were still seated in the crowd, but the chair he'd been in was empty. Then he caught a glimpse of himself, or a body that looked like his, stumbling away from the ceremony. *Am I dying?*

He kept floating. The atmosphere took on a peach-shaded glow. *Is this the bardo?*

A figure appeared, beckoning him, guiding him. The meditator he'd seen on the grass. Aaron immediately felt comforted and cared for. *This being, whoever he is, wants me to be safe, wants everyone here to be safe, wants all the world to be healed from its suffering.*

The peach-shaded atmosphere changed into a glaring sharpness. Aaron felt himself drop and collide with his body, sensing every cell, every atom as he swirled back into it. Dazed, he took a deep breath, then another.

Gravel beneath his shoes. He was leaning against a dirty white truck parked in the driveway beside Timmons House. He looked over and saw that the back door, the main entrance to the Arts Program, was half open. *Who's in there?* He'd seen Viti at the ceremony, and Mitchell as well.

Aaron walked forward, getting acclimated to being back in his body, then stepped inside.

Timmons House was shadowy, even on the brightest of days. Eyes roving, he came upon a massive figure, slumped in Viti's chair, dozing, some object cradled in his lap.

Aaron stepped closer. *Couldn't be.* But it was, no mistaking the red cap, the prominent mole, that appeared in the photo on his glob.

Leslie Kroll had come to Parami and what was on his lap was a shotgun.

Aaron stood frozen, not daring to take a breath.

Kroll's eyes fluttered. His body jerked. He looked around, then looked at Aaron. "Who are you?" he demanded.

Aaron didn't respond, didn't even move.

"Where can I find Elia Adank?" A sour look came across Kroll's already sour face.

"They're honoring him at graduation. I just came from there. Elia . . . wasn't around."

"That oaf doesn't come to his own ceremony?"

"Elia doesn't come to anything."

Kroll nodded. "Thinks he's too good for everybody." A low chuckle. "With what's about to happen, it's better that Adank survives. He'll be blamed and then he'll have to live with it. It's all written up for my glob, just haven't posted it yet."

Aaron felt like making a dash for the door. "What's about to happen?"

Kroll's expression shifted. "Wait a minute, you're that guy on the phone, the one who was so rude to me." Kroll leveled the shotgun. "What the hell is your name? Allen something?" He chuckled. "I guess my secondary target will have to be my first."

Kroll rearranged his weight in the chair, steadying himself.

"Hang on a sec," sputtered Aaron. "Let me get Elia's address for you."

"Why would I want that?"

"He's who you came here for, right? For what he said about the poets of Delaware?"

"That's right," grunted Kroll. "He needs to pay for that."

"You can go straight to his house. I've got his info in my desk."

As Aaron moved toward the smaller room and opened the door, Kroll remained in his chair. "There's no way out of that office, I already checked. Leave that door open so I can see you."

"No problem," said Aaron, forcing an animated, almost cheery voice.

Aaron went to his desk and opened the top drawer and reached in. Papers, pens—the only item missing was the .38 revolver.

Kroll called out, "You're doing something. What are you doing?"

Aaron stood frozen. Kroll raised the shotgun to his shoulder and aimed it at Aaron's chest.

There was not a blast, but a sharp report, and Kroll was sent backwards, a look of consternation on his face. With what he had left, he activated both triggers. The blast was deafening, followed by a silence of a kind Aaron had never experienced. The shotgun tumbled from Kroll's lap, and he leaned forward to pick it up but, as though shoved by some unseen force, collapsed back in the chair. He was still facing Aaron as he breathed in, gasped, then gurgled, the life spilling out of him.

It was a long moment before he averted his eyes but when he did, Aaron saw Nolan Pickering, not in his scarlet bathrobe but in khakis and button-down shirt, standing in the entrance to the Absorption Room, pistol in hand, staring at Leslie Kroll.

"Is he dead?" uttered Aaron.

"Will you take this?" Nolan stepped over and handed the gun to Aaron. Then he reached into his pocket and handed Aaron an envelope. "There's a letter inside. Read it before anybody gets here." He stepped back into the Absorption Room, heading for its side door.

"Where are you going?" Aaron sputtered.

"It's all in the letter. It really helped to write it down. I had no idea there'd be some maniac here, looking to kill you." He turned to go, then turned back.

"You gotta do this for me, Mr. Motherway. If you don't, everything will be screwed, and I need to make things right. You gotta do it."

"Do what, Nolan?"

"Say that you're the one who shot this guy. It's self-defense, you won't get in any trouble."

Nolan rushed out the door.

Stunned and shaken, Aaron stepped back into his office and sat at his desk. The envelope wasn't sealed.

> Hey, Mr. Motherway,
>
> Gonna do like you said & go home. Also gonna tell the truth. See—it wasn't my mom—I'm the one who shot my father! She didn't know he was seeing the ex-nannie—but I did. I felt so messed up I got hold of a .22 & was gonna kill myself—then thought—what am I doing? Planned to shoot them both at our house in Georgetown. But he came out to the country house

before I could put that together. I just lost it that night. My mom said it would ruin my life—so she came up with her prowler story. Only now they're really trying put her away as some jealous killer and that's not fair!! Am going back to tell them everything—if they lock me up I'll just meditate the rest of my life and reach Enlightenment!!! Well Mr. Motherway—you didn't really teach me anything—not like Lawrence Timmons—but then I'm not much of a student

Have your Self a great life!!!!

Nolan P

CHAPTER 42

Homeland Security

Saturday, usually a slow news day, was ablaze with reports about the events at Parami University. Leslie Kroll, a deranged individual, had been killed by a single shot to the head, delivered by faculty member Aaron Motherway. A truck loaded with explosives was parked at Parami, and Kroll had a fuse that would have activated the blast, annihilating everyone attending Parami's graduation ceremony, as well as all in the surrounding area.

Aaron saw all this recounted with dizzying repetition on local and national television and, as the day unfolded, became aware of the throng of reporters outside his apartment building. Among the sequences that kept running was an interview with Betsy Cohn, standing on the spot where Kroll's truck had been parked.

"It's a tragedy what happened," she declared, "no two ways about it."

"Wouldn't it have been more of a tragedy," the female reporter asked, "had Aaron Motherway not been prepared to spoil Leslie's Kroll's diabolical plan?"

A look crossed Betsy's face, something between empathy and annoyance. "It would have been handled differently, had it been almost any other member of the Parami community. Unlike Aaron Motherway, most of us have Mindfulness training and we could have talked to Mr. Kroll and made him see that—"

Aaron turned off the television and silenced his cell phone. He peeled off his clothing, climbed into bed, and awoke midafternoon on Sunday.

The media was still out front. Aaron switched on the television and was freshly reminded that he had killed Leslie Lawrence Kroll, fifty-nine, of Wilmington, Delaware. Wyoming State Senator Garrett Landis appeared over and over, saying he would be hosting an event at Pearl Handle's Hotel Raphael, Monday at 8:00 p.m., to promote: "The Motherway Initiative, which will mandate that all Wyoming educators, both in public and private institutions, undergo weapons training, and be in possession of a firearm at all times while at school."

Aaron turned the TV off for good.

Monday evening, a few minutes before eight, he put on a sport coat and tie and, for the first time since late Saturday afternoon, stepped outside. The media were taken by surprise. A young male reporter said, "Where are you going, Aaron?"

Aaron hadn't glanced at him or anyone else until he turned to the guy. "Give me a ride, and I'll tell you."

THE CONVENTION ROOM at the Raphael was bright and teeming with people. Garrett Landis was at the podium as Aaron came in, flanked by several reporters.

"The educators are the good guys," Landis was saying. "So are the employees at theaters, as well as the workforce at fast-food restaurants and shopping malls. Any bad guy turning up to do harm at a school—or a public place conducting business—should be taken out, no questions asked, exactly as that bona fide Wyoming hero, Aaron Motherway, did."

At that moment, one of Landis's aides stepped up and leaned close to the senator. Landis looked eagerly around the room.

"Speak of an angel, I've just been told that none other than the namesake of our initiative has just arrived. Aaron, where are you?"

There was a tremor, then an explosion of applause as Aaron strode onto the elevated stage. Beaming, Garrett Landis moved toward him, only to have Aaron sweep by and go straight to the microphone. The applause peaked, and when it trickled down, Aaron stood looking at the crowd.

A long moment, then someone shouted, "Talk to us, Aaron!"

Another moment. "You're the man, Aaron!"

Aaron, dazed and awkward, somehow found his voice.

"First of all, I'm not a hero. I had a gun only because it had been dropped or discarded and I happened to come across it. If anyone here thinks I feel good about shooting someone, you're sorely mistaken. That's still a heavy burden to carry." He glanced over at Garrett Landis. "Anybody who thinks it's easy has never gone through it.

"Am I glad there was a gun on hand when Leslie Kroll turned up on the Parami campus? I am, or a great number of innocent people, myself included, wouldn't be around today. But do I propose, as Mr. Landis is attempting to legislate, that every teacher and administrator, in every school, that the entire state of Wyoming carry firearms?" He turned again toward Landis, who was now glaring at him. "That's where he wants to take this, some return to the Wild West that has more to do with an ambitious politician looking to widen his constituency.

"So, no, don't call me a hero. I don't feel anything like a hero. And be sure to take my name off your ridiculous initiative."

Silence in the room. Somebody called out: "What's next for you, Aaron?"

Aaron took a moment. "I'll probably go back to Hollywood, where people who've never had so much as a playground fight keep spewing violence all over the screen, thinking it's sexy."

As Aaron left the podium and reached the side of the stage, a couple of men closed in on either side of him.

"We'd like a word with you, Mr. Motherway."

Aaron, not looking at them. "I've said all I'm gonna say."

"We don't think you have."

The one who'd not been doing the talking stepped in front of Aaron, who stopped moving and said, "Is this is about the restraining order?"

IN THE STERILE hotel meeting room where Aaron was escorted, a woman wearing a navy skirt and blazer had taken charge.

"So, Mr. Motherway, were you to make a formal deposition, your statement would include that the money you took possession of, on behalf of Parami University, was duly deposited in the institution's Conscious Credit Union?"

"That's what I was told."

"By whom?"

Aaron looked around, as though seeking reinforcements. "I don't think I should say anything further without having an attorney present."

"Why would you need counsel? You're not being charged with anything." The official, who had not so much as provided her name, smiled for the first time.

"We're with Homeland Security, Mr. Motherway. Since 9/11, anytime more than ten thousand dollars is withdrawn from—or deposited or transferred to—a financial institution, we're obliged to investigate. Eight hundred thirty-two thousand, one hundred twenty-five dollars being moved around is bound to get our attention. Do you know anyone who might have been desperate enough to need to get their hands on that amount of currency?"

Aaron's mind jumped to Madlenka, the staff member who'd called him seeking to ferret out petty cash, and of whom Harold Black Kettle said he'd never seen anybody lose so much money in such a short time.

"You've gone pretty quiet," the interrogator said. "Is there something you're not telling us?"

Another moment. "Like I said, I want a lawyer."

"You're not a target, Mr. Motherway, we consider you a resource."

"And what exactly does that mean?"

The woman glanced at her associates, then said, "Would you be willing to testify against Parami employee Madlenka Kovacs, as well as university President the Reverend Doctor Stamford Moses?"

Moses? Aaron mind was reeling.

"Why wouldn't you?" the interrogator continued. "Although total amateurs, those two were clearly trying to set you up."

WHEN AARON RETURNED to Los Angeles, he got his belongings out of storage, reclaimed his aged but restored Jaguar, and moved back to Los Feliz. He did end up hiring a lawyer, but only to settle what his former insurance company claimed he owed them.

On the internet, he kept up with events related to Pearl Handle, Wyoming.

Ophelia Jenks (Opal) married Hank Gaffney, who, on their Las Vegas honeymoon, suffered cardiac arrest and died. Prior to the private wedding chapel ceremony, Opal convinced the renowned sculptor to alter his will so that the whole of his estate would go, not to the establishment of an artists' colony in Montauk, but to Opal herself.

After Nolan's plea of accidental homicide, Beverly Pickering announced that, in advance of his trial, she would be marrying the attorney who championed her case and who would now be defending her son.

Viti Balakrishnan submitted a chapbook to the International Poetics Foundation and was awarded a lucrative three-year stipend as America's Most Promising New Poet.

When Roger Bayne Whitney announced that plans for Parami becoming a "faith-based university" were being scrapped, the Reverend Doctor Stamford Moses stepped down as Presider. This was shortly before he was charged with embezzlement, along with Madlenka Kovacs.

Parami named Betsy Cohn interim Presider. She promised to return the institution to its mission of delivering Mindful Instruction. Announcing that Parami's Chamber of Wisdom would reassume its original nonplural designation, she named as its Archon, Philip Pristley. She further stated: "Parami University, with its unwavering commitment to renewal and compassion, will not support the prosecution of Reverend Doctor Stamford Moses. Nor will Parami bring charges against Madlenka Kovacs, an immigrant, single woman who naively fell victim to a number of decadent aspects particular to this country's debased and materialistic culture."

And that figure meditating on the grass, who Aaron was convinced had somehow drawn him out of his body—*Who was he and where had he gone?*

One morning, Aaron's cell phone chimed.

"Aaron Motherway, Roxie Herman, senior editor at—"

"What can I do for you?"

She laughed. "What else, write a book."

"I don't have any—"

"A memoir, about what you got caught up in out in Wyoming. It's gold, Aaron, priceless."

How much gold, how priceless? "I'm not sure I want to revisit—"

"Everybody in the house is already on board. Do you have an agent, or shall I tell you directly about the whopping advance we have in mind?"

A moment. "I'll need to think about it."

"Not for long, okay? You know what they say about food left on the counter. It tends to spoil."

Aaron did consider it, for a week.

"Whaddaya say, Aaron? The clock's ticking."

"If you need an answer . . . it isn't yes."

"But is it no?"

"No, it isn't no."

"What's your resistance? I don't get it."

"A memoir? I'd have to tell the truth."

Roxie laughed. "Nobody tells the truth in a memoir."

The following week. "What's the word, Aaron, have you come to your senses?"

"Still thinking."

The week after that. "I have to have an answer. Everybody's tugging at my sleeve."

Aaron took a breath. "I just don't wanna go back and look at all that stuff. So, the answer is no."

A long sigh on Roxie's end. "You're gonna regret this, my friend."

One middle of the night, some feeling took hold of Aaron and he rolled out of bed, consumed with creative flashes of the kind he'd only experienced when he conceived *The Sell Out*. He went not to his computer but to the freezer, yanked out a nearly full bottle of Tito's, then filled a tall glass.

Sitting at the keyboard, Aaron felt one of those inspired glimmers lifting, then lingering.

Mind empty, his fingers fluttered over the keys.

Like most institutions of higher learning, Parami
University was a world unto itself . . .

ACKNOWLEDGMENTS

Gratitude to: editor Deborah Gibson Robertson, publicist Mary Bisbee-Beek, and book and cover designer Karen Sheets de Gracia.

Further gratitude to: Lisa Birman, Lawrence Block, Steve Cowan, Sharon Fiffer, Bhanu Kapil, Tom Leavens, Rocky Maffit, Stuart Oken, Alan Rosen, Louis Rosen, Dana Walden, Laney Wax. And of course, Michele Leonard & Simone B. B. Leonard, there for every step.

ABOUT THE AUTHOR

Junior Burke's *The Cold Last Swim* (Gibson House Press, 2020) was one of five finalists for a Sidewise Award, the annual prize for novels of Alternate History. His short fiction was included in the anthologies *Litscapes: Collected US Writings 2015* and *Collectibles*, published in 2021. He lives Out West.

GIBSON HOUSE PRESS

connects literary fiction with curious and
discerning readers. We publish excellent novels by
working musicians and musicians at heart.

GibsonHousePress.com
GibsonHousePress
@GibsonPress
@GHPress

READING GROUP GUIDES AVAILABLE:
GibsonHousePress.com/Reading-Group-Guides